THE HELL'S ANGEL KIDNAPPING

When a sixteen-year-old girl is snatched from her bed at night as a hostage by an intruder, Detective Sergeant Scamp's prime concern is to safeguard the victim's life. The father cannot be trusted to co-operate with the police for fear that his daughter will be killed. The dilemma for Scamp is whether to compound a felony by allowing the father to buy back his daughter's life for a ransom, or whether to try to outwit the kidnapper and the father together, thus putting the girl's life in greater danger.

P. A. FOXALL

◆

THE HELL'S ANGEL KIDNAPPING

Complete and Unabridged

LINFORD
Leicester

First published in Great Britain by
Robert Hale Limited
London

First Linford Edition
published 2005
by arrangement with
Robert Hale Limited
London

British Library CIP Data

Foxall, P. A.
    The Hell's Angel kidnapping.—
    Large print ed.—
    Linford mystery library
    1. Kidnapping—Fiction
    2. Detective and mystery stories
    3. Large type books
    I. Title
    823.9′14 [F]

    ISBN 1–84617–113–X

Published by
F. A. Thorpe (Publishing)
Anstey, Leicestershire

Set by Words & Graphics Ltd.
Anstey, Leicestershire
Printed and bound in Great Britain by
T. J. International Ltd., Padstow, Cornwall

This book is printed on acid-free paper

1

'Have you ever tackled a kidnapping, Scamp?' said Detective Inspector Earwacker.

'That's not our type of crime, is it, guv?' said Detective Sergeant Scamp uneasily. 'Italy's the place for kidnapping. It's just not on over here, except in Ireland, where they're all bloody mad.'

'Well, stand by to lose another of your cosy illusions,' replied Earwacker grimly. 'Kidnapping is now the crime of the century, and we can't expect to be immune. In fact we've got one right here on our patch, just landed on my desk. It's only suspected at the moment, but it smells like the real thing to me. I could be wrong, of course.'

When Earwacker conceded that he could be wrong, it was the most positive assertion that he knew he was right, and Scamp's heart sank accordingly.

'What's the starting price then, guv? Is it just for money, or is there a political motive? Who's the victim?'

'A sixteen-year-old girl, Alison Norman. Her father is Donald Norman, owner of Norman Plastics in New Cross. He's loaded, by all accounts, so it looks like a bid for a ransom. There's been no demand yet. She only went missing last night from the family home in Court Lane, Dulwich.'

'Isn't it a bit premature to assume kidnapping then?' said Scamp. 'At sixteen she could be out on a bender, or playing house with some athlete.'

'No, she's not the type. According to her schoolteachers she's a quiet, serious-minded little thing, studies hard for her 'A' Levels and is an accomplished pianist. She attends an Independent Day School for Girls at Sydenham, and is driven there and back every day by her mother. She's always lived a sheltered life, hardly ever allowed out on her own, pampered and indulged, as you'd expect the only child of doting parents to be. She disappeared from her bed in the middle of the night, and she didn't walk out alone. Somebody broke into the house and took her away by force.'

'Is that positive, guv, or just an educated guess?'

'There are no signs of breaking and entering, according to preliminary reports. But the house could easily have been entered through a downstairs sash window whose catch was released by a knife blade. Also there's an ornamental stone archway at one corner of the house, just underneath a first-floor balcony. Anybody with some agility could have shinned up there and hauled himself straight into a main bedroom. The shutters were open, and the window left ajar for ventilation. The girl wasn't given time to dress properly. Just her overcoat over her pyjamas and a pair of outdoor shoes was all she took. Presumably the kidnapper made her walk downstairs and out through the front door, which opens on an ordinary yale lock. No dead bolt on any of the outer doors, or safety bolts on the windows. Your average citizen's idea of security gives all the drummers an easy living.'

'Who was in the house at the time?'

Only the mother, her daughter and a resident housekeeper. Mr. Norman was away from home on a sales mission in Belgium, and you can bet the kidnapper knew it. The mother says she was woken up at about two o'clock by a single sharp noise. She thought it was one of the others going to the bathroom, so she thought nothing of it and went back to sleep. She agrees it could have been the sound of the yale lock snapping shut as the front door was closed from the outside.'

'She didn't hear a car start up?'

'Nothing as straightforward as your kidnapper driving straight up to the front door in a taxi,' said Earwacker sardonically. 'I'd like you to go over to Court Lane and take on the investigation. The local constabulary are in charge at present, and no doubt will give you every assistance. The mother is distraught, so use your best bedside manner with her. The father should have been notified by now and will be on his way back from Belgium. If we don't crack this in the first few days, our chances of getting the girl back alive will be down to zero. So let me have any lead you find, however feeble, and we'll follow it through. I'm going to get permission from the Home Office to have the house and factory telephones monitored for when the kidnapper makes contact.'

He scribbled down the address of the Norman house in Dulwich and handed it to Scamp. Two minutes later Scamp, accompanied by Detective Constable Burgess, was driving out of the motor pool in an unmarked C.I.D. car bound for Dulwich.

This new and formidable case was one which he could well have done without. The business brought in by his usual customers, the thieves, gangsters, dope pedlars and perverts was as brisk as ever and had to be kept going. There was never any question for him of a lull before the storm. After the summer of political rioting and industrial punch-ups on the London streets, in which Scamp and his peers had become increasingly resigned to being regarded as enemies of Society, there came the annual Notting Hill

Carnival, always an excellent opportunity for the disgruntled failures, psychopaths and anarchists to crawl out of their holes and have a go at the police. Then came the convivial week-end hooliganism of the football season, in which a copper's only permitted function was to be a sacrificial goat for the high-spirited youth.

When the unaccustomed crime of a kidnapping was handed to him, with the danger to an innocent hostage causing imponderable complications at every step, Scamp realised with stoic fortitude that he wasn't going to come out of this with any medals.

Donald Norman's house stood magisterially in two acres of lawn and shrubbery. Its broad and rather flamboyant red brick façade faced south-west. The wrought-iron balconies on all the first-floor windows were bright with trailing pelargoniums in ornamental boxes. It all looked too compact and well groomed to be anything but the single accommodation unit of a prosperous family.

There were a couple of police cars

parked in the drive, and Scamp introduced himself to Detective Inspector
Bolton of the Dulwich C.I.D., who'd
taken provisional charge of the case.

'I don't mind telling you this is one
case I'm glad to hand over to the experts,'
he said with relief. 'There's absolutely
nothing to go on. No footprints in the
flower-beds or palm prints on the window
frames. Nobody saw anything. There's
been no rain for a week or two, so we
found no tyre marks on the drive. That
girl just vanished into thin air. In fact I'm
starting to wonder if she's an amnesia
victim who just walked out on her own,
not knowing who she was or where she
was going.'

'Let's hope it is like that,' said Scamp.
'If she's just roaming the streets in her
pyjamas and overcoat we'll have her back
by tonight.'

'Thank God the bloody newspapers aren't
on to it yet!' exclaimed the Inspector.

'How's the mother bearing up?'

'Gone completely to pieces. She's got
plenty to say, but it doesn't add up to
much sense.'

Accompanied by D. C. Burgess Scamp walked into the imposing entrance hall of the house, with its statuary and antique treasures and its dark old oil paintings that looked as if they'd been varnished with gravy. A uniformed police constable on duty showed them to a small chintzy sitting room at the back, where the distraught mother was alone with her grief.

Margaret Norman was a big-framed woman in her forties who dressed in the square old way with tweed skirts and twin sets and ropes of pearls. Her grey hair was untinted and cut unpretentiously short. Her comfortable curves showed that she valued good food more than high fashion. She was now completely demoralised, her face puffy and tear-stained, her swollen red eyes blinking short-sightedly without the accustomed spectacles. She sat in an easy chair, rocking herself and keening like some bereaved old peasant woman at her cottage door, clutching to her bosom a leather vanity case as if her life depended on it.

'Oh God,' she cried as Scamp introduced himself. 'Still more of you asking the same questions. When are you going to stop talking and *do* something? My baby is in the hands of some vile beast, and all you policemen can do is hang about here asking me stupid questions. She gave me this case for my birthday only a week ago, and now she's gone. I know I shall never see her again. She was all I had. I couldn't have any more children.'

She was off again, racked with hysterical sobs, hugging the vanity case as if her life depended on it.

Scamp gestured to D. C. Burgess to get lost in the hope of putting her more at her ease.

'Mrs. Norman,' he said soothingly, 'I understand how you must feel. We're going all out to find your daughter. Every policeman in London will be looking. But we've got to have somewhere to start, and that means here, with all the information you can give us.'

'Why?' sobbed the woman. 'Why should it happen to us? We never did

9

anybody any harm. My husband was always a good employer. He helped those less fortunate than himself. Nobody had any cause to injure him.'

'We're going to look closely at all his employees and commercial associates,' said Scamp. 'But there are other angles as well that we can't ignore. Did Alison have any boy friends who could have lured her away?'

Mrs. Norman froze in starchy indignation and gulped back her sobs.

'Certainly not. She was only a child at school. She was too keen on her studies and her music to waste any time on that sordid adolescent nonsense. She went everywhere with us.'

'She was — I mean is — sixteen,' rejoined Scamp, 'emotionally and physiologically a woman. As there's no evidence of the house being broken into, could she have slipped out to meet somebody when she knew you were asleep?'

'How dare you!' exclaimed the woman, giving him a venomous look. 'My poor child is to be blackened and vilified to make your responsibility less.'

'Not at all. I know my responsibilities. We'll find your daughter. You can be sure of that. The only worrying thing is how long it's going to take.'

'Well, Alison has not gone off voluntarily with any man,' declared Mrs. Norman vehemently. 'She went to bed at ten o'clock last night, a normal happy schoolgirl. I looked in on her at half past eleven when I went up, and she was sound asleep, without a care in the world. This morning when she didn't get up for school, I thought she'd overslept. I went up to wake her with a cup of tea. When I saw her empty bed all disarranged, her wardrobe wide open, coat and outdoor shoes gone, I collapsed, because I knew somebody had been in and taken her away by force. There couldn't be another explanation.'

'Don't you have a dog?' said Scamp.

'Not now. We did have one for fifteen years, but when it died my husband didn't want another. He said it caused too much sadness to have an old friend put down when the time came.'

'I'm told the only other person in the house last night was your housekeeper.'

'Yes, Nancy. Miss Robson.'

'I shall want to talk to her. Is that a picture of Alison on the mantelpiece?'

'Yes, but that was taken when she was only twelve. Her latest picture is on the piano in the music room.'

She struggled out of her chair and left the room to fetch a framed, coloured photograph of a dark-haired round-faced girl, not particularly good-looking and rather sulky. Her features bore a certain immature resemblance to Mrs. Norman's. It wouldn't be long now before that picture was on the front page of every newspaper in the land.

Scamp went into the kitchen to tackle the resident housekeeper, Miss Robson, a fat, red-faced, bucolic woman with legs like tree-trunks. She was dressed in a dark blue maternity smock, but you couldn't tell whether she was pregnant or not under the protective folds of obesity. Unlike most fat people she was morose and unsmiling.

'Miss Robson?' queried Scamp.

'MIZ Robson!' she retorted fiercely, putting the chauvinist pig in his place.

He asked her about her job, and she soon let him know that she wasn't particularly keen on her employers or the job itself.

'I just do the cooking and catering and cleaning up after meals,' she said tartly. 'When the daily woman decides to take a day off, I work a sixteen-hour day. That's the worst of a resident post. You're always on call. I mind my own business, and I'm not treated as one of the family. The Normans are a funny lot.'

'Funny in what way?'

'Not friendly, stand-offish, what I'd call close. Mrs. Norman checks the house-keeping money every week, and wants every penny accounted for. She's got nothing else to do but molly-coddle Alison. Mr. Norman's never hardly here.'

'How did you personally get on with Alison?'

'I never saw much of her,' replied the housekeeper disdainfully. 'She wasn't encouraged to be friendly with the domestics. When she wasn't at school, she was practising on the piano, or up in her bedroom doing her homework, or watching television. She was too quiet for my liking, too wrapped up in herself and spoilt. Her mother followed her about, picking up and carrying for her. Anything she wanted she had. She took a week off school last June to watch the tennis at Wimbledon.'

'Did she ever bring any friends here?' said Scamp.

'I shouldn't think she had any friends,' replied Miz Robson. 'Too spoilt and moody was that little madam.'

'How long have you known the family?'

'I've been here a year, and I don't mind telling you I'm on the look-out to be better suited.'

'Oh?' said Scamp. 'Did you know your predecessor, Miz Robson?'

'No, but I heard she was fired and left in a hurry. Some trouble over Alison, and she'd worked here for twelve years.'

'Do you happen to know what sort of trouble over Alison?'

'The Normans want it kept dark,' replied Miz Robson. 'But May Bodle

— she's the daily woman — reckons it was something to do with Alison having a boy friend on the quiet.'

'Amazing,' said Scamp.

'Yes, isn't it! Especially when you look at the plain little thing. It's the quiet, shy ones you've got to watch. I'm making sure the crafty little bitch never lands me in any trouble.'

'She's landed in enough of her own, by all accounts,' observed Scamp. 'Do you believe that somebody broke into the house and took her away by force?'

'I never heard anything last night,' replied Miz Robson. 'But then I wouldn't, would I? Sleeping up on the second floor in the servants' quarters. If somebody did come in and take her away, I reckon it was one of them Arab Sheiks with his white slavery. Buying up all London, they are, and everybody knows they like to take English girls back home better than race-horses.'

'No doubt,' said Scamp. 'But what about this alleged boy friend who got the other housekeeper fired?'

'You ask Mrs. Norman about that, and

don't tell her I mentioned it. Nobody's supposed to know what sweet little Alison got up to when she wasn't playing her piano.'

Scamp went back to the grieving mother and started again.

'I understand Miss Robson has only been with you a year,' he said.

'That's right.'

'Would you care to tell me about your previous housekeeper?'

Mrs. Norman bristled at once with defensive indignation.

'Helen Webster? What about her? How can she have anything to do with finding Alison?'

'It's a possible line of enquiry,' replied Scamp. 'How long was she with you?'

'Eleven or twelve years.'

'Oh, then she must have watched Alison grow up.'

'Obviously,' retorted the woman, tight-lipped.

'Was she a sort of nurse companion to Alison, as sometimes happens with a faithful retainer of long service in a family?'

'No,' snapped Mrs. Norman. 'I didn't approve of my child being influenced by domestics.'

'Did the woman leave here of her own accord, or was she sacked?'

'She was dismissed.'

'Oh?' said Scamp. 'May I ask why?'

'It was — oh well, it was a question of dishonesty.'

'What sort of dishonesty?'

The woman's hands were shaking and she was obviously on the verge of another hysterical outburst.

'How can this matter?' she protested. 'How can it possibly help Alison now? The woman stole a gold bracelet belonging to Alison. She was accused and admitted the theft and gave back the article. She preferred instant dismissal to having the police called in. Are you satisfied now?'

Scamp knew instinctively that the woman was lying, but he didn't wish to harass her further in her present state. He would get at the truth by other means later on.

He left Mrs. Norman and had a quick

look through the rest of the house, where the finger print men were still hopefully checking doors, sills, window frames and banisters for alien finger and palm prints.

He had a quick look in Alison's bedroom which was at the front of the house with lovely parkland views towards the College and its playing fields and the several sports grounds and golf course. From here you wouldn't have thought it was anywhere near the centre of a vast conurbation.

The bedroom had been the prime target of forensic examination. Even the carpet had been tested for alien footprint impressions, and samples of its dust swept up in a portable vacuum cleaner in the hope that the intruder had left significant occupational traces.

The room itself was a typical young girl's bedroom, brightly furnished and lavishly endowed by the gifts of affluent parents: transistor radio, hi-fi equipment, guitar, portable colour TV set, writing desk and typewriter. Significantly there were none of the posters of hirsute pop stars and other recipients of adolescent hero-worship adorning the walls. The book shelves contained school text books and rather heavy novels, the reading of a prim and serious-minded young girl.

The bedclothes were still in the position where they'd been roughly flung back, and the wardrobe door from which her overcoat had been taken still stood wide open. Scamp had a brief vision of the petrifying terror the young girl must have endured when she awoke in the dead of night, face to face with some ruthless criminal.

He went back downstairs to compare notes with D. C. Burgess, who had been busy talking to the Normans' jobbing gardener, Ted Bodle, and his wife May, the daily cleaning woman.

'I'm particularly interested in the former housekeeper, Helen Webster,' said Scamp. 'I want to know why she was fired after twelve years' service. Did the Bodles let on about it?'

'They were quite happy to have it extracted,' said Burgess. 'About a year ago Alison had a brief, furtive romance with a garage attendant where they stopped for petrol on the way to school. They'd give each other the eye behind the old woman's back — strong mutual attraction — and on his day off this forecourt attendant would hang about the tennis courts while Alison was playing there. The poor little over-protected rich girl must have been quite bowled over at having a real live admirer. They started sending notes and having secret meetings. Alison got round the housekeeper to cover up for her one night while she went canoodling with Romeo. The woman was to leave a back door unlocked so that Alison could sneak back without her mother knowing. But Mrs. Norman wasn't fooled so easily. She found out about the whole con-spiracy. Mrs. Webster was fired for her immoral influence, and poor old Alison couldn't even go to the tennis courts afterwards without Mummy standing in as chaperone.'

'It's probably not important,' said Scamp, 'but we'd better not let it go. I want this garage Romeo found and thoroughly checked. Even if he's got no criminal inclinations himself he could have some family connection or nasty acquaintances who wouldn't be above spotting the potential of the Norman girl for a heavy and easy ransom. There can't be all that many petrol filling stations between here and Alison's school in Sydenham, so get on to it. After that, you can check on Miz Robson, the present housekeeper. She's probably got a man somewhere in her life.'

'You're thinking about the child's nurse in the case of the Lindbergh baby?'

'Just tidying up loose ends,' replied Scamp. 'I'm going looking for the former housekeeper, Helen Webster. I want all her male connections run through the computer.'

'You think she could have a revenge motive, getting fired from here?'

'Who knows?' said Scamp thoughtfully. 'If this were a straightforward bid for a ransom, surely the intruder would have left a note behind in the house, warning them not to bring in the police and telling them to wait for instructions. The fact that the snatcher is saying nothing, just letting the parents sweat with uncertainty, shows a deranged or sadistic streak, obviously a nutter.'

'Maybe she died on him,' suggested Burgess uneasily, 'choked on her gag or something.'

'That wouldn't affect the plans of a bastard like this. He'll still go for the money eventually, even though he's only got a dead body to trade.'

'If it's revenge as well as money he's after,' mused Burgess, 'we're going to have to check out all the employees past and present at Norman's factory, not to mention all the enemies he's made on his way up.'

'I know,' said Scamp. 'So what are we hanging about here for?'

2

By the evening of the first day there was still no news of Alison Norman or any communication from the kidnapper. The Back Room Inspector at Scotland Yard responsible for press releases decided to reveal the basic facts to the news media. The picture of Alison was flashed on all TV channels and published in all the national dailies under the caption:

MISSING FROM HER HOME
IN DULWICH

There was an urgent request for information from anybody who might have seen her. The police were concerned for her safety, and did not rule out the possibility of foul play.

Scamp started looking up his snouts in all the pubs, street markets and doss houses for any possible whisper of underworld activity against Donald

Norman that may have leaked on to the sub-community's grapevine. But nobody knew a thing about the Normans, and the facts surrounding Alison's kidnapping were a completely closed book. It looked as if the kidnapper's amateur status could be protecting him. As he had no professional criminal contacts, no informer could betray him.

The forensic examination of the house in Dulwich hadn't yielded a single alien finger print, though there were scratches from a knife blade on the catch of a sash window in the kitchen, which showed where the kidnapper had entered the house.

The Yard's latest infra-red equipment had raised the imprint of a size nine shoe with flat soles on the carpet of Alison's bedroom, and that was the only data they had on the criminal.

As soon as he heard that Donald Norman was back from Belgium, crazed with grief and anger and threatening untold sanctions against Scotland Yard if they didn't bring his daughter back safe and well, Scamp went back to Dulwich on the unpleasant errand of interviewing the outraged father.

Donald Norman was not an easy man to confront at the best of times. He was in his late forties with a bulky and muscular body. His face was strong-featured and well-fleshed, with intense, challenging eyes in deep sockets. He always assumed a squat, square stance with his jowls stuck out like a bullfrog. His clothes were expensively tailored and in the best of taste. His manner was imperious and arrogant as became a prosperous and forward-looking factory owner. He had influential contacts to go with his wealth, and as Detective Inspector Earwacker had already warned Scamp, he was a man to be treated with discretion.

Norman loved his only daughter with a stern and proud possessiveness, even though he didn't have much time to see her, and he regarded her abduction as a personal affront that he wasn't going to stand for. He glared at Scamp, the six feet two detective who looked like a guardsman in civvies, much as a fastidious bird fancier would regard a tatty old crow.

'So it's come to this now,' he snarled. 'None of us can sleep safely in our beds any more. We're over-taxed, over-governed and over-policed, but our children can still be snatched from their homes in the middle of the night. Well, I'm warning you, if a hair of that child's head is harmed, there's going to be hell to pay. I belong to the same club as a Chief Superintendent from the Yard and a First Secretary from the Home Office. I'll make damned sure you people do what you're paid to do, protecting life and property and civil order. This damned country gets more like America every day in all the worst aspects.'

'I suppose I'd feel exactly the same if my daughter was at risk,' replied Scamp, trying to keep his cool at the man's offensiveness. 'We'll find Alison, but we're going to need your frank, whole-hearted co-operation as well. No more half-truths, cover-ups and downright lies for the sake of some misdirected respectability.'

'What the hell are you getting at?' demanded Norman angrily.

'I'm referring to your wife's deliberate lying to us over the sacking of your former housekeeper, Helen Webster. We had to spend extra man-hours and trouble to find out about Alison's teenage romance with a motor mechanic, time needlessly wasted that could have been better spent on the main enquiry.'

Norman was taken aback, and for a moment looked almost chastened, but he soon recovered his bluster.

'Wouldn't you expect a mother to be sensitive about her daughter's good name?' he snapped. 'I suggest you're trying to use a young girl's momentary indiscretion as a red herring.'

'As it happens we've already traced the youth concerned, Harry Pettinger of Bromley, and we're satisfied he's a harmless lad who had nothing to do with the kidnapping. But you get the point about vital time being lost through your lack of frankness. We need a quick break-through to get Alison back unharmed.'

'Oh, very well,' said Norman ungraciously, finally abandoning his attempt to intimidate Scamp. 'I have nothing to conceal. Ask all you want. I'll try to give full information.'

'Let's go to your factory now then, and we'll check every name on your payroll. I want to know about all the awkward customers, those with a grievance, those with personal animosity towards yourself or your firm, those who've been dismissed in the past five years for any reason whatsoever. Above all I want the names of those you've taken on, knowing them to have a police record. There's also the question of your own personal enemies, political, business and social. I want complete frankness here, or the whole thing is a waste of time. Don't suppress any run-in you've had just because you're ashamed of the part you played and would rather forget it.'

Norman looked uneasily at his watch. It was past nine o'clock in the evening, less than two hours since he'd arrived home from Heath Row. He'd only just had time for a hurriedly prepared meal, and he was tired and demoralised. He certainly didn't fancy spending hours at the factory, mulling over grievances past and present of his work force with this grim looking and apparently indefatigable policeman. But the thought of Alison alone, terrified and in mortal danger from some vicious criminal gave him new reserves of stamina. He went immediately with Scamp to his factory in New Cross, and was admitted by the night watchman.

Upstairs in his office, together with the Personnel Officer who'd been urgently summoned from his home, he and Scamp sat till two in the morning, going painstakingly through the employment register and the confidential file on every employee at the factory, preparing a short list from two hundred men and women of those who were thought to have it in them to snatch the boss's daughter for greed or revenge.

Finally they narrowed it down to five outstanding probables, men whose track records gave Scamp cause for rapid search and investigation.

Barber and Holman were political activists who'd been dismissed as trouble-makers a year ago, when they'd tried unsuccessfully to bring a trade union into Norman's factory. As Norman paid wages above union rates and had a largely satisfied work force, who didn't want union shop stewards fomenting unrest and costing them money in lost production, the agitators had failed to get a strike going and had paid the penalty of failure. When they took Donald Norman before the Industrial Relations Tribunal for unfair dismissal, their claim had been rejected. So now they were wounded and embittered men, who nursed an implacable hatred for Donald Norman.

Fairbrother and Bradshaw, who had police records for shop-breaking and theft, had been dismissed six months ago for stealing sheets of laminated plastic with which they were building their own boat in their spare time.

Finally there was Thomas Henwood, a man of unpredictable and explosive violence, who'd attacked a foreman and beaten him to the ground when he was told off for loitering over his tea break. Henwood had served six months in gaol for the assault, which had taken place more than two years ago. He'd been taken down to the cells, loudly swearing vengeance on the foreman for victimising him and on Donald Norman for firing him. But nobody had seen or heard of him since. He'd certainly never been back to Norman Plastics, and if the kidnapping of Alison was his act of vengeance, he'd taken his time over planning and executing it.

Scamp immediately got in touch with the divisional police at the last known addresses of the five men and asked for a check on their activities, especially any further indictable offences they'd committed.

Predictably Barber and Holman, the two political activists, were still active. They were currently remanded on bail for obstructing the police and insulting behaviour on the picket line of a North London factory in its dispute with a trade union.

Of the two thieves, Fairbrother was currently serving an eighteen-month sentence for burglary, and Bradshaw was working on a new construction project in Saudi Arabia.

Thomas Henwood the man of violence had disappeared from his lodgings in

Peckham some months ago after a long period of unemployment, and nobody knew where he'd gone. As he'd been brought up in an orphanage, was unmarried and completely alone, he was a difficult man to trace. He was also very well placed to hold a prisoner without anybody knowing. Scamp asked for a general alert to bring him in, for Henwood was the only possible suspect to date.

Meanwhile, as a matter of priority, Scamp sought out the address of the sacked housekeeper Helen Webster as soon as he could, and went looking for her at her crumbling basement flat in Lewisham. There was no answer to his knock, and he noticed that two full bottles of milk were sitting uncollected on the cracked and greasy doorstep.

As there was no resident landlord in this unsavoury tip to come and open up the flat for him, Scamp used his policeman's license to force an entry through the kitchen window. The damp, miserably furnished flat was in disarray, as if the occupant had left in a hurry.

There was dirty crockery in the sink and the remains of a hastily consumed meal on the table. In the bedroom the drawers and cupboards were wide open with some dresses, coats and shoes still there. She'd gone so precipitately that she hadn't been able to take all her clothes.

Scamp made some enquiries among the other tenants in the building, and found the consensus that nobody had seen Helen Webster since Saturday. This meant her rapid and demoralised disappearance virtually coincided with the press release of Alison Norman's suspected kidnapping. It was as if she feared she was one of the first people the police would want to interview in connection with the kidnapping.

Scamp now had a strong hunch that in some way Helen Webster was crucial to this case, and he had to find her. The Normans couldn't help. They'd washed their hands of her a year ago. Scamp put out an instant alert to have the woman picked up and brought in for questioning. But the official police procedure was obviously going to be slow in this case, for

Helen Webster didn't want to be found.

When he was looking for a reluctant witness or guilty absconder, Scamp generally had somebody in the relevant district on whom he could rely for information. In this case it was an Egyptian hotelier called Gamal Kanafi who ran the Hotel Byzantium in darkest Lewisham. It was a tall, gloomy place in a run-down district with a crumbling façade, a refuge for illegal immigrants, taxi drivers and petty thieves. The basement, whose grimy windows looked out on a noisome courtyard, contained a refreshment counter that never closed. It also served as a temporary resting place for homeless drifters and a convenient venue for whores, banished from the streets, to meet their clients. They paid the Egyptian a royalty on each trick they turned.

Gamal Kanafi, who owed Scamp something for trapping an Arab black-mailer bleeding him to death, was a large fat man with a face as smooth as lard and a drooping black moustache. He always dressed with nationalistic fervour in red

34

fez and cummerbund. He'd lived in London since 1945, quietly amassing a fortune with his wide ranging fiddles and business deals. Nobody knew the full scope of his contacts in the seamier strata of the multi-racial society.

Scamp didn't come to see him very often because he couldn't afford the time. A visit to Gamal Kanafi generally entailed the red carpet treatment, with a banquet in Arab style. Scamp had to sit cross-legged on a mat and dip his fingers in a congealing mutton stew, from which the sheep's eye glowered up at him malevolently. Kanafi watched him like a hawk to make sure he took the supreme delicacy of that leering eyeball on which the guest had first preference. To have refused it would be considered a mortal insult.

After the banquet came an exhaustive game of chess, which Kanafi always won. Having invested a couple of hours in this routine, Scamp finally got round to telling Kanafi of his problem of the whereabouts of Helen Webster. The Egyptian got on the phone to one of his countrymen, a notorious ponce called Mustapha Amsor, whose speciality was the racing form and availability of all the bedworthy women in Lewisham.

'The woman Helen Webster once had a bad husband,' reported Kanafi.

'Oh?' said Scamp. 'Bad in what way?'

'He is a thief, a no-good, a bum who gave her a hard life. He has been in prison.'

'Well, that's always a good place to start from,' observed Scamp. 'Anything else?'

'His name is not Webster. That is the woman's unmarried name.'

'Do you know her husband's name?'

'They have not lived together for many years. When she lost her residential post a year ago, she came to Mustapha looking for work to supplement her Social Security. He could not do anything for her. She is too — how do you say it — down market at her age. But he is keeping her in mind for the back end of the trade at bank holidays, when any woman is a woman.'

'Does he know why she's suddenly disappeared from her flat without taking all her belongings?'

'It is probably because her husband has come back. What else? But if you must talk to her, Mustapha will have ways of knowing where she is, for a small research fee, of course.'

'Of course,' said Scamp. 'I'll buy it.'

So Kanafi put him in touch with Mustapha Amsor, an evil-looking, hatchet-faced Egyptian with a black shade over one eye. (His parents had followed the well-known Egyptian Fellaheen custom of putting out one eye of their first-born son so that he would not be eligible for compulsory military service.)

Within twenty-four hours, on the payment of twenty pounds, Scamp was given an address in a small hotel called The Norfolk, situated in slum bed-sitter and small hotel country in Blackheath.

At nine in the evening the proprietor in his green baize apron and collarless shirt shivered furtively at the sight of Scamp's warrant card. He confessed eagerly that he had a single woman guest answering the description of Helen Webster, who'd taken a room three days ago with hardly any luggage. She'd signed in as Mrs.

Curtis with an address in Manchester, and she spent all the time in her room without visitors. She was there now, alone.

Scamp went up the narrow carpeted staircase to the second floor and knocked on her door.

'Who's there?' said a woman fearfully.

'Police,' said Scamp briefly. 'Open up.'

She was a tall, rather faded woman in her forties who had once been very good looking. But now she had a pale, mask-like face and eyes of a peculiar glassy emptiness that looked as if all the grief had been washed out of them. The Normans' former housekeeper was dressed conventionally in a green two-piece suit that looked creased and travel-stained. Her flat comfortable shoes were old and down at heel. Scamp looked round the stereotyped, impersonal hotel room and thought that whatever life had brought her along the way, it was obviously neither happiness nor prosperity.

'Mrs. Webster?' said Scamp.

'My God!' she gasped. 'How did you know?'

'You were housekeeper for twelve years to the Normans in Court Lane, Dulwich. You left your flat in Lewisham as soon as the news was released that Alison had disappeared. You're hiding here under an assumed name. Would you care to tell me why?'

The woman wept hysterically.

'I was afraid,' she sobbed. 'I couldn't face the police and all the newspaper men. I knew they'd be after me. They'd think I hated the Normans because I was sacked unfairly.'

'Did you hate them?'

'I never hated Alison. But I didn't think much of Mrs. She was a silly spoilt woman, with nothing better to do than go about the house finding fault and fussing over Alison.'

'Yet you stayed there for twelve years.'

'Well, it was a good home for somebody like me who never had one. I felt secure there.'

'So it came as a nasty shock when you were dismissed?'

'What do you think? And it was over nothing, a silly prank of Alison's. She talked me into covering up for her while she sneaked out to meet some lad.'

'I'm not suggesting you had any crazy scheme for getting your own back by abducting Alison,' said Scamp. 'But what about somebody close to you who knew the circumstances? Your husband, for instance.'

Mingled emotions of fear, anger and resentment flashed across the woman's face.

'I wondered how long you'd take to get to him,' she exclaimed. 'The last thing I heard of him he was in prison. I haven't seen or heard from him since I went to keep house for the Normans thirteen years ago.'

'I gather Webster is your maiden name?'

'My word, you're quick! Well, I wasn't going about boasting I was connected to *him*, was I?'

'So what is your husband's name?'

'Hansler. Jack Hansler. And he could be dead for all I know. I haven't seen him from the day they took him downstairs from the dock and left me a grass widow.'

'Why did you run for cover as soon as you heard that Alison could have been kidnapped?' pursued Scamp. 'Did you think it could be your ex-husband?'

'No, but I knew you lot would think it was, and be after me like a shot, trying to get at him. I was right, wasn't I?'

'We have to eliminate him from our enquiries. What did he go to prison for?'

'Theft and fraud. Cooking the books, that was his style. He thought any employer was an exploiter and fair game for being robbed.'

'Was he a violent man?'

'No. He just drank and backed horses. He never raised his hand to me in the three years I lived with him. He was just weak. I realised when he'd gone down that I wasn't missing much. Thank God we had no kids.'

'So you don't think it possible that if he got desperate enough for money, he could have planned and carried out Alison Norman's kidnapping?'

'Of course he couldn't! He wouldn't know where to start. Even if he took her from her bed, he'd get drunk and let her escape.'

'Do you know any of his associates who

would do it?' said Scamp thoughtfully. 'Anybody in his family or on your side of the family capable of an outrage like this? I can tell you we shall be looking very hard at Hansler's C.R.O. file and his whole family tree. There's a young girl's life at stake here, so we shan't pussyfoot around.'

Helen Webster was on the verge of hysterics again.

'You've made your mind up it's got something to do with me, haven't you?' she sobbed. 'But I can't tell you anything. I'm sorry for Alison, but I've got to feel sorry for myself as well, haven't I? I can see I'm not going to get any peace, whether Jack Hansler's in it or not.'

Scamp deliberated a moment. He had that certain feeling that she knew more about the case than she was letting on. She was frightened of something and she was definitely holding back information. Perhaps there was some other man in her life whom she judged capable of abducting Alison, but she was too frightened of him to give his name.

'If you ever had any affection for

Alison,' said Scamp, 'I urge you to help us find her. Can you imagine what she must be suffering even now, probably bound and gagged in some dark, filthy hole at the mercy of a brute?'

'Please go away and leave me alone,' sobbed the woman. 'I can't help you, and you're making me feel awful. Of course I can feel for Alison. I knew her when she was three, and watched her grow up. She used to come in the kitchen to talk to me when her mother wasn't looking.'

'I may as well spell it out,' said Scamp grimly. 'If Alison should die in captivity and it turns out that you withheld vital information which could have saved her, you'll be facing a very serious charge.'

The woman looked terrified and started weeping again. But Scamp was convinced she knew something which, probably from motives of misplaced loyalty to somebody she was refusing to divulge.

In spite of her tears and desperate pleas he made her go back with him to Squad H.Q. in Bermondsey, where he and Detective Inspector Earwacker spent more than two hours interrogating her. Though broken and despairing and racked by sobs and hysteria, she would reveal nothing else, apart from what she'd already told them about her ex-husband Jack Hansler.

In the end, feeling frustrated and uneasy with a sense of impending disaster, Scamp laid on a squad car and driver to take her back to her miserable hotel room in Blackheath. At midnight in his office he received the C.R.O. file on Jack Hansler, and prepared to work through the small hours.

The file on Hansler was fairly stereotyped, but interesting in a nasty way. He was the bent cashier type, the falsifier of accounts and plausible con man, who saw it as a matter of principle to rob his employers blind, and to screw money out of lonely women by spinning endearing lies. Having read the fifteen indictments and eight convictions against him in the past fifteen years, Scamp was convinced that Hansler's ex-wife had been telling the truth. Jack Hansler was a pathetic thief and twister, definitely not the type to break into a house and abduct a teenage girl from her bed. But with his track record he could easily be involved with some harder villain who was capable. He had to be found at once and all his associates thoroughly screened.

Scamp spent the next two hours ringing up the various police stations in the metropolitan area where Hansler had once been charged. His last prison sentence had been served three years ago — eighteen months for passing dud cheques — and his last known address was a bedsitter in Brockley. He'd moved from there two years ago and the local police had lost track of him. There was nothing else down to him as far as they knew, and they expressed surprise that he was wanted for questioning in connection with the kidnapped girl.

3

At four o'clock in the morning Scamp was still sitting in his drab, ill-ventilated office, assailed by small-hours depression, reflecting that even then people were being hounded, tortured and murdered within a mile's radius of where he sat. But somehow because it was impersonal it all seemed trivial compared with the forcible imprisonment of one sixteen-year-old girl, whom Scamp was beginning to know very well.

At last, totally exhausted, Scamp went home to his bachelor flat in Southwark for three hours' sleep. He was up again at seven thirty with the disciplined punctuality of a man attuned to doing two hours on and four off in a guard-room. By nine o'clock he was shaved and breakfasted and back at his desk in Bermondsey, checking through a batch of reports from well-meaning citizens and cranks who claimed to have seen Alison Norman in widely divergent parts of London.

He wrote up his report on the interview with Helen Webster and the search for her husband. Then he set out to interview a villain in Deptford on another case he was working on.

When he arrived back in the afternoon, the phone was ringing and an irate Detective Inspector Earwacker was gunning for him.

'Scamp, why the hell didn't you keep that Webster woman in custody?'

'On what grounds, guv? You saw what a state she was in, and we couldn't get any more out of her. You agreed she's just an ordinary poor sort of woman, not likely to be involved in the kidnapping. It's the ex-husband we want, Jack Hansler.'

'The hell she's not involved!' roared Earwacker. 'She went straight back to that doss-house after you so considerately released her, and killed herself with a massive overdose of sleeping pills.'

'Oh my God!' muttered Scamp aghast. 'When did you hear that?'

'It just came through from the Information Room at the Yard. The

47

Norfolk Hotel in Blackheath. A Caucasian woman in her forties, registered as Curtis. She didn't come down to breakfast. She wouldn't answer the phone, and her door stayed locked all morning. The manager was worried in view of your visit last night and her returning in a hell of a state after midnight. He went in and found her. She'd been dead for some hours. She must be mixed up in the kidnapping somehow, or she thinks she knows who's responsible. As soon as you flushed her out she knew we'd go on leaning on her till she told us everything, which she was determined not to do.'

'She probably suspected her ex-husband was implicated somehow, and dreaded the shame of her association with him,' said Scamp. 'We shall know more about it when we pick up Hansler. I've got just about everybody in the Met. looking for him.'

'Well, we haven't got all that much time left,' fumed Earwacker. 'The A.C.C. is getting worked up about this case. Donald Norman's got friends in the House of Commons, probably with company directorships in his firm. Work it out. If something doesn't get moving on this case soon, they'll give it to Tintagel House. You know how Superintendent Hickman's going to like that.'

He slammed the receiver down, and Scamp blasphemed to himself, knowing that D. I. Earwacker and all the brass above him were more concerned over personal loss of face and rebuke and censure from the media than over the sufferings of a sixteen-year-old girl who had now been in evil captivity for four days, assuming that she was still alive.

* * *

Having received a promising phone call from his most reliable snout, Scamp was sitting in Battersea Park, waiting to meet him there. Scamp sat as unobtrusively as possible behind a newspaper on a seat overlooking the boating lake, watching young children and their mothers feeding the ducks in the crisp, bright autumn sunshine. He kept looking out anxiously to make sure that no villain had followed him there. It was one of the endless little games that detectives always had to play with the sub-community. The snout was extremely sensitive about the risks he ran in selling information to Scamp, knowing he was a dead man if any of his peers suspected he was a grass. He refused point blank to meet the detective in any public place such as the clubs, wine bars and street markets of South London, for there was always some sharp-eyed bastard lurking where he hadn't ought to be. The meeting had to be in an open space like a park or a common, where hoodlums and their hangers-on were not eager customers for fresh air and communion with nature.

The snout was more than half an hour late, but Scamp waited, knowing his man. He'd come all right, unless he'd been done in since making his phone call that morning.

The snout's name was Titch Shaw, a scrawny runt of a man five feet two in his platform shoes, who ran a small newsagent's shop in the Old Kent Road, known as The Hole in the Wall. Titch

Shaw had been inside a few times for burglary, and he made no secret of the fact that he'd opened his shop on the proceeds of crime.

He'd been an army band boy in his youth, and was generally known as Titch the Trumpeter. This name stemmed from a famous escapade of his, just after he left the army with a dishonourable discharge. Having got plastered one night, and feeling extra sorry for himself, he stood in the middle of Highgate Cemetery at two o'clock in the morning and sounded Reveillé on his trumpet, keeping the living residents in the entire district awake, until he was hauled away by the indignant constabulary and bound over to keep the peace.

Presently Scamp saw him sauntering along South Drive, unmistakable in his flashy suit and gangster's fedora hat. He had a wrinkled, leathery face a bit like a lizard's, and bright, flashing, mercurial eyes. He stood on the edge of the lake for five minutes, looking warily all round him, and then came over to sit on Scamp's seat.

'Morning, guvnor. Anything new?' said the snout.

'Nothing to rejoice about,' replied Scamp, which was what Titch Shaw always liked to hear.

'I got something for you very tasty,' said the snout. 'You'll really like this, guv.'

'I hope so,' rejoined Scamp.

'You know that face Tom Henwood you asked me about? You fancied him for snatching the Norman girl. Well, I don't think he did, 'cause I know where he is, and he's in the money all right. Must have come up on the football pools about the same time as that wages snatch in the Blackwall Tunnel. Remember that, guv?'

'I remember,' said Scamp. 'It's still on the file, but we never got anywhere. There's one of the security guards still in a coma with brain damage and his eyes burnt by ammonia.'

'A pub called The Goat and Compass in Camberwell,' said the snout. 'Henwood's got a room there. He's well in with the landlord, Steve Herd. You know him?'

'Can't say I have that pleasure.'

'You bleedin' well ought to,' replied the

snout. 'He's a hard bastard and he's done time.'

'How can he be the licensee of a pub then?'

'Licence is in the name of his old lady, Edie, innit? Steve Herd's in the money as well. They must have a syndicate going for that football pool divi they won. They're always chuckin' it about in Archie's Club, down Peckham way. I've seen 'em there with one or two other faces that I couldn't put a name to, well dressed and hard and spending money like they printed it. Makes you sick, dunnit, when honest mugs like us got to graft like blacks for it.'

'It's certainly worth knowing,' conceded Scamp. 'We'll pay them a visit.'

'Better make it fast, guv, or the buggers will have spent it all. Steve Herd's got a lock-up garage at the back of The Goat and Compass. Always got this bloody great padlock on it, as if he's thrown away the key. I had a shufti through a crack in the door when I was round there, guv. That's all I know. Looks like a van or a Land-Rover. Them hoods used a stiffed-up

Land-Rover to ram the security van, didn't they?'

'That's right, and it disappeared into thin air after the blag. We'll certainly get moving on it.'

He handed over a couple of five-pound notes which the snout grabbed hungrily, spat on for luck, and tucked away in an inside pocket. He made no attempt to go, but sat there ruminating for some minutes, after which he glanced sideways at Scamp and said: 'You know that business about Norman's girl being snatched?'

'Yes?'

'Nobody knows nothin'. It has to be an out of town job, nothin' to do with any London firm. One thing I heard though, you might like to hear about. Years ago, when he was first getting his factory going, Norman had a run-in with Charlie McCann.'

'What kind of a run-in?' said Scamp sharply.

'The usual. Anybody employing labour had to deal with Charlie McCann.'

'But Norman never had the union in his factory. He always paid over the odds

54

to keep them out.'

'Keep 'em out! You can't keep them buggers out. McCann's hoods were in Norman Plastics, breaking up his machines, weren't they? But Norman wouldn't give in. He brought in the police and got McCann done for it. McCann went to stir, a two-year stretch, and when he came out he was finished with the union. Set up in business on his own and never looked back.'

'Is that it then?'

'Yeah guv. That's it. It's worth a couple of oncers innit?'

'Why?'

'You're looking for some berk who wants to get back at Norman, and snatched his girl to learn him. Well, there's one for you, Charlie McCann, a real hard case, and Norman had him put in stir. McCann's the type as takes no shit from nobody. He could bring in some hood from Glasgow to do a quick snatch and out again, without dirtying his own hands at all, or anybody sussing it.'

'Well, it has some possibilities, I suppose,' said Scamp thoughtfully, and gave the little snout an extra quid to keep him happy.

He strode back to his car and returned to H.Q. to organise an immediate swoop on Thomas Henwood and his accomplices at The Goat and Compass. Also he had to study the form of Charlie McCann. It was always good practice to follow up hard on a criminal lead, even thought he didn't really believe that Charlie McCann would soil his hands by kidnapping a child.

McCann was a former dockers' union official turned company director. He'd come on a long way since his start as a brawling shop steward in the East India Dock. After doing time for extortion and conspiracy in the course of his ideological warfare on employers, he'd given up struggling for the betterment of his brothers and gone into business on his own account. The source of his wealth lay in some crafty Long Firm frauds and a few highly successful robberies, for which retribution had never overtaken him. Now he was so far above the average thief and hoodlum as to be an Establishment figure and, as far as the police were concerned, an untouchable. If he did occasionally fancy an easy-money rip-off to buy a few more high-priced antiques, he hired a professional fixer who did all the research and planning and hired the muscle men to do the job on the ground. Then, if anything went wrong, the mugs who were nicked did their time with sullen stoicism, the fixer was in Morocco, and there wasn't so much as a gossamer thread linking the blag to Charlie McCann. It was a pattern all too familiar in jackpot London these days, and all the detectives were pissed off about it, except those who were earning handsomely from the situation.

Scamp went to visit this scion of the newly rich in his luxury flat overlooking Green Park. A velvet smooth lift with electronically operated doors whisked him up to the fourth floor, and a suave, old-world English butler with a supercilious upper lip and a smarmy manner ushered him into a splendid lounge thirty feet square, with a snow-white carpet and gold damask hangings as a backdrop to the costly antique furniture which McCann was crazy about.

Charlie McCann, dressed like a playboy in white safari suit, dark blue silk shirt and foulard knotted Western style, was watching the nags at Newmarket romp home on the TV screen. He was an over-indulgent, slack-bodied man with a red boozer's face and a huge domineering nose. He had darting lively little eyes like a mouse's, and his fleshy fingers, once so used to the feel of brass knuckles, were now adorned like a pouf's with costly jewelled rings.

He greeted the detective deferentially, with wary eyes and a slight unease, wondering what should come down so heavy in his irreproachable life, for he'd heard of Scamp by reputation even though their paths had never crossed.

'What's the problem then, Mr. Scamp?' he asked innocently.

'The Norman kidnapping,' said Scamp bluntly. 'I hear you and Donald Norman were the best of enemies twenty years ago, when you were in the union ram-rodding business, and Norman preferred non-union labour. In fact he got you put away for extortion and criminal damage in his factory, didn't he?'

'So what does that do for me now, Mr. Scamp?' said Charlie with deadpan eyes.

'His girl's been snatched. He hasn't been told a damned thing since it happened. Nothing. Somebody's out to have him frying on the griddle. Wouldn't you say it's somebody with a grudge?'

'It could be, but screwing money out of the bastard would be my guess. Anyway, it's not my style, if you're working on that angle, Mr. Scamp. If I wanted to get back at that prick Norman, d'you think I'd have waited twenty years? D'you think I'd do him over proper, or get at him through his little girl? You know my form, so which d'you reckon it would be?'

'I have to admit it's not your style,' agreed Scamp thoughtfully. 'But sometimes people act out of character, just because they know it's going to fool the opposition.'

'Do me a favour,' scoffed McCann. 'I admit there were times in stir when I could have really gone up the wall for bloody Norman. I wanted to cut his balls off and string 'em up like salami. But in the end I realised he'd done me a good turn. It was in stir I met the blokes with good connections who put me on the right road to the top. Before I could be anything, I had to get rid of all this worker solidarity shit and brotherhood of man. So when I came out — with full remission, Mr. Scamp — I was raring to get started building up my life by the new rules. I couldn't care less about Norman any more, or his bloody exploited workers. I couldn't be bothered to piss up his kilt if he was on fire, and I wouldn't cross the road to put the boot in if he was flaked out in the gutter. As for kidnapping his girl, only a flaming nut case would take that on. I mean, all the trouble of snatching the mark without killing it or getting identified by it, the sweat of arranging the pick-up two moves ahead of the fuzz, and then the worry of having marked money to spend. You know what it costs to get dirty money laundered these days. You get back fifty per cent, if you're lucky. What a hell of a way to get a living! Don't quote me on this, but I'd rather snatch a pay-roll any day, if I was lookin' to score. It's easier and more flippin' honourable.'

'I believe you,' said Scamp. 'You're known as an honourable villain in that respect. But I had to eliminate you from my enquiries.'

'Well, no hard feelings, Mr. Scamp,' said Charlie magnanimously. 'You coppers are doing a grand job. And just to make sure you ain't had a wasted journey here, I'll give you a tip-off about Norman to make you realise just what a lousy bastard you're wasting your grief on. Years ago, after I come out of stir, I heard Norman framed his wages clerk and had him put away, just because he was balling the bloke's wife and wanted her to himself.'

'Well, that's something worth knowing,' observed Scamp, 'if it's true.'

'You'll find it's true all right, plus a good few more of Norman's dirty tricks, if you dig deep enough.'

'Do you remember the man's name?'

'No, it was nothing to me. But Norman

took care of the wife after, signed her on as his housekeeper so he'd got it always on tap, the dirty bastard.'

'Well, well,' said Scamp, 'now you're starting to make a lot of sense, Charlie. I won't insult you by offering you the couple of quid, standard information fee for unsolicited help.'

'What d'you mean, insult me?' snapped Charlie McCann. 'Gimme. I'll snatch your hand off for two quid from the fuzz any day.'

★ ★ ★

As soon as he got back to H.Q., Scamp put one of the best D. C.'s Geoff Burgess, to research into the background and activities of Jack Hansler. The investigation substantiated much of what Charlie McCann had said.

'But I don't go along with the framing accusation,' said Burgess. 'Hansler came to work for Norman as wages clerk when he'd already got form. Norman must have had rocks in his head to put him in charge of the accounts department.

Hansler started fiddling and kept it going for years as the business expanded, to finance his secret night life, boozing and gambling. He was into Norman for thousands before he was found out. Naturally the police were called in and Hansler went down for five years. His house was sold up by the building society, and Helen Hansler was left with just a few sticks of furniture and nowhere to live. Whether Norman was balling her or not is anybody's guess, but he certainly took her into his house as housekeeper, where she stayed for twelve years, until that famous little bust-up over Alison's boy-friend a year ago.'

'I wonder why Norman never told us about all this,' mused Scamp.

'Maybe he's a bit ashamed. Maybe there's something else even more embarrassing or incriminating that he doesn't want us poking about in.'

'I sometimes wonder if he ever wants to see that girl again at all,' said Scamp irritably. 'He's not falling over himself to help us, is he? We have to dig everything out the hard way. I think I'll go over to his factory and ask him what the hell's going on.'

'D'you want me in tow?'

'No. Stay with the Hansler story,' said Scamp. 'It gets more fascinating by the hour. Keep digging and see what else you can turn up.'

Scamp took an unmarked car and drove out to the Norman plastics factory in the industrial working class district of New Cross. The modern factory buildings sprawled like aircraft hangars in a raw open space backing on to the railway. New tower blocks and old grey areas of decaying back-to-back terraces alternated with building rubble and active development sites.

At Norman Plastics the pungent and repellent stink of petro-chemicals and synthetic resins hung heavy in the air, as delivery vehicles, company cars and fork-lift trucks darted all over the factory area, making life hazardous.

Donald Norman was in his executive suite making swift sharp decisions, making his underlings jump and scuttle about, losing himself in the whole-hearted exercise of power. His heavy, jowly face darkened with sullen pain as he saw Scamp and was forced to remember his daughter's plight.

'Well?' he demanded with asperity. 'Is there any news of Alison yet?'

'We've not found her, and your less than hearty co-operation is not helping matters.'

'What the hell do you mean? I've told you everything I know with any bearing on the case.'

'Have you now? Well, for instance, why did you see fit to suppress the significant fact that Jack Hansler, thief and gaol-bird and former employee of yours, was once married to your housekeeper, Helen Webster?'

Norman was visibly shaken by this approach, and had to pour himself a drink.

'How did you know about Hansler?' he muttered.

'We have means of turning up background information, especially in a case like this where the clue to the kidnapper's identity might well lie in your background. I'm getting a bit fed up with your secretiveness and obstruction, Mr. Norman. It's your daughter we're trying to find, and you seem to have forgotten that she's in danger.'

'Not Hansler,' muttered Norman. 'I don't believe that. He bore me no malice. He understood it was Hibberd, the company secretary, who found out the embezzlements and called in the police. I promised Hansler I'd look after Helen while he was away, and I kept my word. Why would he do this to me, twelve or thirteen years later? I know he's not the type. Hansler is the last man on earth to be violent.'

'You should let us be the judge of that. Why didn't you even mention him to us?'

'I don't know,' replied Norman defensively. 'Perhaps I was embarrassed and wanted to forget him. You see, Helen Webster and I — well, she was my secretary before she married Hansler. Well, you know how it is. She and I were lovers. But Hansler never knew. It was over between us by mutual consent before I took her on as housekeeper and gave her a home. She was just another employee then, and accepted her status.'

'Did she have any children, to your knowledge?'

'She had one that was still-born in the first year of her marriage. I think it could have been mine. There weren't any more.'

'You know that she's dead?'

'Yes, I heard. I'm very sorry.'

'She'd run away from her flat and gone into hiding under the name of Curtis. It was the news of Alison's kidnapping that drove her into hiding. When we traced her she was terrified, almost as if she knew something or thought she was about to become involved. She may have suspected her husband. Or do you know of anybody else in her life whom she might be justified in suspecting?'

'I've no idea,' muttered Norman, starting to look harassed.

'Do you mean you're really no idea, or are you covering up something else embarrassing?'

'I honestly don't know. She lived with us quietly. She never had any men, as far as I knew, after losing her husband in prison. She was glad to lead a sheltered domestic life.'

'And yet you suddenly threw her out a year ago. It was a harsh and brutal dismissal if I've heard it right.'

'Yes, well, that was my wife,' retorted Norman shamefacedly. 'A difficult, neurotic woman. She'd found out about Helen and me in the past, and always held it against her. When she saw a justifiable excuse to sack her for duplicity, she made up her mind that Helen had to go. Nothing I could say would change her mind. In the interests of domestic harmony I had no choice. You understand?'

'Our enquiries are still centred on Hansler,' said Scamp, 'and if he or his associates should get in touch with you, you must let us know at once.'

'Of course,' replied Norman meekly.

'We're monitoring your incoming phone calls and vetting your mail, both here and at your home. If the kidnappers should communicate with you by some other means, I trust you'll call us immediately and not try dealing with them on your own. That way you could lose the money and the girl.'

'I understand,' said Norman dispiritedly.

'If a suspicious-looking letter is delivered by hand, remember we shall want to examine it for finger prints. It's true most criminals have heard about finger print identification and usually take precautions. But there's always the odd case where they forget in the general excitement of a criminal's life, and that's the only bonus we get.'

4

On the fifth day the kidnapper broke his silence with a phone call to the Norman home. The detective on watch timed the call at nine thirty in the evening, and it came from a public call box. The voice was disguised by speaking through a handkerchief stretched over the mouthpiece. It was brisk and articulate, with no regional accent or class inflections, probably belonging to a man in his twenties or thirties.

'Are you there, Norman?'

'Yes, Donald Norman speaking.'

'You fascist bastard! What does it feel like to lose something you value? How do you like being robbed, you bloody robber? What shall it profit a man to exploit a work-force and lose a daughter?'

'Oh my God!' gasped Norman. 'You mean Alison? Are you — is it you who took her? Is she all right?'

'Shut up!' snapped the caller brutally.

'She's not tied up or gagged, is she? She's delicate and easily frightened. This is a terrible experience for her. When will you let her go?'

'Shut up, I said, and listen. She's still alive. How much longer she stays like it depends on you.'

'Anything you say. I'll do anything,' babbled Donald Norman abjectly. 'Please set her free and send her back to us. It's a traumatic experience that could damage her for life, being locked up. Her mother would never survive the shock if anything happened to Alison.'

'All the more reason for you to cough up then,' replied the other callously. 'Seventy-five thousand in cash. Our firm doesn't take rubber cheques. Why only seventy-five thousand, you may wonder, from a bandit with all your assets? The answer is it's the biggest sum that can be conveniently transported in bulk in notes of small denomination. I want no brand new printed fives, tens or twenties with serial numbers in sequence that can be easily traced to the spender. I know all about the fuzz technique. And comradely greetings to you fellow criminals in blue who are no doubt listening in on this conversation. You'd better not try baiting any traps, like marking the ransom money or following it to the dropping zone, or the girl could become a dead issue. There's no way round me. So wait for the next call, Norman.'

'Wait!' pleaded the father desperately. 'How do I really know you are the kidnapper? This could be another cruel hoax. We've had several calls already from sick and malicious people pretending that they have Alison.'

'Oh, I've got her all right,' said the caller grimly. 'I'll send you a little token of recognition. What would you like, an ear or a finger? I'll put one in the post for you.'

He gave a malicious little chuckle and rang off.

Margaret Norman who'd been listening to the call on an extension telephone went into hysterics and had to be tranquilised by a heavy input of valium.

★ ★ ★

Informed of this new development, Scamp and Detective Inspector Earwacker sat in the latter's office, playing back the cassette recording of the telephone call, listening carefully to every syllable, every inflection and turn of phrase.

'This is no hoaxer,' said Scamp. 'It sounds as if he knows all about Norman and hates his guts. So it is somebody from Norman's past life who got trampled on in Norman's ascent. The kidnapping is an act of vengeance as well as greed.'

'Slow down. You're way ahead of me,' growled Earwacker. 'Just because he calls Norman a fascist, a bandit and a bloody robber, that doesn't signify a lifelong hatred. It's standard trade union and student jargon for any businessman who makes a quid or two.'

'You think he could be a student then, guv?'

'He talks like one. Probably some self-righteous college boy radical, who's crossed the hazy line from political fanaticism into crime. Everything can be justified by political sophistry. He doesn't sound like some pig-ignorant East End tearaway. But then you've got expressions like 'cough up' and 'fuzz' and cutting off an ear or a finger which do suggest the criminal community.'

'Then you've got his reference to the Dropping Zone,' countered Scamp, 'which means he could once have been a paratrooper.'

'Very funny,' said Earwacker morosely.

'And what about his biblical quotation: 'What shall it profit a man?' '

'So he's a rogue parson now,' scoffed Earwacker.

'Let's say student (query). Age group, twenty to thirty, with a decidedly warped sense of humour and a streak of sadism. If he was serious — which God forbid! — about sending an ear or a finger to identify Alison by, he's also a bloody psychopath. I asked Norman if he recognised the voice, but it was so distorted speaking through cloth that he couldn't tell. Not that I'd trust that bugger to give us any help. We're trying to get back his daughter for him, and he's as shifty as any villain.'

'What the hell are we going to do?' said

Earwacker peevishly. 'Do we just wait, hoping the girl's all right, and leave the initiative to this swine?'

'I'd like to have Norman under surveillance without his knowledge,' said Scamp. 'I don't trust him to go along with us when the kidnapper gives him directions for making the drop. I know we've got all his phones tapped and his incoming mail sewn up. But we've no means of intercepting a note smuggled in by hand to Norman at the factory, warning him under dire threat to bring the money alone and leave us out of it. The kidnapper knows we've got the phone tapped, and he won't want us muscling in on the pick-up, so he'll intimidate Norman into servile co-operation. From what I've seen of him so far, I think Norman is the kind of B.F. who'd rather trust the kidnapper than us with his daughter's life.'

'You could be right,' conceded Earwacker grimly. 'All right then. Full surveillance on Donald Norman until something breaks. Is there anything else we can do?'

'I'm still working on the Hansler angle, mainly trying to find him as well as his relatives and associates. Also I'm trying to find out what happened to Helen Webster's sister who went to Australia. Did she ever come back to this country, and did she have any children? The kidnapper is not only someone who knows the Norman family well. He's also well informed about their movements. He knew for instance when Mr. Norman was away from home on a trip to Belgium, and it was safe to break in and snatch Alison without a soul seeing anything.'

★   ★   ★

The following morning at five-thirty while it was still dark, a motor cycle with a black-clad rider, black leather jacket, black boots and black helmet, with goggles and scarf over his face, came roaring down Court Lane to the Normans' house. As he approached the gateway he braked violently and tossed a parcel tied up with string and brown paper into the drive. Then he accelerated away, his exhaust note shattering the pre-dawn silence of the stately suburb.

Almost before the young detective constable keeping surveillance on the Normans' house from his parked car was aware of what had happened, the black-clad rider had disappeared into Lordship Lane and down London Road. Taking full advantage of the empty streets, he roared south at eighty miles an hour, jumping red lights with impunity. He was long gone by the time the startled detective had radioed the news to the R.T. room at Squad Headquarters. Only an impregnable road block system immediately activated all round Dulwich could have stopped him.

'What kind of motor-bike was it?' said Scamp, patiently questioning the rather red-faced detective, who'd been made to feel that he'd blown his assignment in failing to stop and hold for questioning the demon motor cyclist.

'I don't know, skipper. It sounded like one of these big Japanese jobs, 750 or 1000 c.c. The back mudguard was chromium plated. I just caught a flash of it in the street lighting.'

'What about the rider? Did he look big, small or medium?'

'He was so hunched up over the handlebars, I wouldn't like to say.'

'You said he was all in black, from black helmet to black boots. Did you notice anything else about him?'

'Come to think of it, skipper, he looked a funny shape, as if he'd got very wide black trousers on, or even a black skirt. Here, it couldn't have been a Judy, could it?'

'No,' replied Scamp, 'this one's no Judy. But I'm glad you noticed the black skirt.'

The brown paper parcel, carefully examined by the Yard's Forensic Laboratory, was found to contain a girl's navy blue overcoat, identified by a name tag sewn inside the collar, as the coat that had gone missing with Alison. In one of the side pockets was a long lock of dark brown hair which the Norman's promptly recognised as belonging to Alison. So here was the incontrovertible proof that the black-clad motor cyclist was indeed the criminal who held her prisoner.

Microscopic examination of the returned coat revealed several black dog's hairs clinging to the woollen fibres. There were also clusters of eggs laid by the dog's fleas, as if Alison had been in actual close contact with the hound.

The hairs were identified by canine experts from the Dog Handlers' Section as the hairs of a Dobermann Pinscher, one of the most ferocious and remorseless of all guard dogs used by man. Alison's terror, held in close contact with such a killer beast, could well be imagined.

The dust extracted from the overcoat contained traces of very old ground flour and bran, which prompted the speculation that she was being held captive either in some old flour mill, stable or warehouse. Whether it was some old storage depot along the Thames, or some disused water mill out in the country was anybody's guess. It would take years to search every derelict mill and warehouse in London, never mind those in the southern counties outside London.

'So now we know our man is a leather-jacketed Hell's Angel, who's got the girl locked up in some deserted flour mill, guarded by a Dobermann Pinscher,' observed Earwacker morosely. 'And that doesn't inspire confidence in any easy solution. It just rules out the possibility that Alison could ever escape.'

5

Alison Norman had been petrified with terror when she was roughly awakened by a cold gloved hand over her mouth and the sight of a horrific black hooded figure dimly outlined in the distant glow from the street lamps through her window. The cold blade of a knife was laid against her throat, and she could feel the tingling sharpness of the honed edge ready to pierce her flesh.

'Get up!' hissed the intruder. 'Put this on, and your shoes. One sound and you're dead.'

She hurriedly put on her school overcoat and the outdoor shoes he handed to her. Unable to speak, in a kind of catalepsy of terror, she let him guide her silently past the bedroom door and along the landing, down the broad stairway and out through the front door, which her captor carefully closed behind him. There wasn't a soul in the quiet road to help her or witness her abduction as she was hustled along to a dark, nondescript van, waiting a few yards away from the Normans' driveway entrance. Alison was bundled inside through the back doors, still with her captor's gloved hand clamped over her mouth, and the dark figure of the driver, also hooded, started up and drove away.

After the first hideous shock of terror, when she realised that she had been kidnapped and was being taken to an unknown destination by ruthless assailants, Alison knew the agony of complete despair. She burst into panic-stricken sobs.

'What do you want with me? Please don't do it,' she pleaded. 'Let me go. I won't say anything.'

'Shut up!' snarled her captor, giving her a cruel jab in the ribs.

The driver still hadn't uttered a word, but Alison was already beginning to suspect from a faint whiff of expensive perfume wafting back at her that the hooded driver was a woman. For some strange reason Alison was immensely cheered by this discovery. She didn't feel so much alone. She fondly hoped that one of her own kind would mitigate whatever evil was intended towards her. Another woman would never go along with the extremes of male cruelty and outrage being practised on her. Of course it was only money they wanted. She knew her father would gladly pay up any amount to get her safely home. So there was no real reason why she shouldn't be treated in a civilised manner after the initial brutal shock of her seizure.

As the van cruised rapidly through the deserted South London streets, she tried to observe and memorise the route they were following. But the male kidnapper suddenly realised what she was doing, and roughly tied a black scarf over her eyes, pushing her down on the floor of the van so that she couldn't see anything.

After about an hour's driving, the hum of the tyres changed to a harsh crunching sound and the van lurched heavily as they left the metalled road surface, turning off on what must be a stony track or unmade road.

The van stopped and her two captors got out, dragging her with them. She felt she was standing on the cobblestones of a courtyard, and the intense, eerie silence without the familiar background traffic noise of London told her she was in the heart of the countryside. A cold autumn wind suddenly sprang up, struck through her overcoat and flimsy nightdress, and she realised for the first time that she was chilled to the marrow.

Suddenly the silence was shattered by the deep-throated baying of a large hound that chilled her blood with a new terror. As she was hustled, still blindfolded over the slippery cobbles, she could hear the savage panting of the dog and the frenzied scraping of his claws on a closed door as he strove to get at her.

Soon she found her feet rustling through straw, and there was the unmistakable leathery, musty smell of a coach-house or stable where horses had once been kept. She was made to ascend a steep flight of wooden steps on to the floor above, which consisted of several rooms, probably store-rooms and even living accommodation for long dead ostlers and coach-men.

Alison worked it out that she was being incarcerated in the outbuilding of some big house buried deep in the country, where her screams for help would never be heard.

The man who'd taken her from her home removed the blindfold from her eyes, and for the first time she saw him plainly in the pale light of the hurricane lamp he carried. He looked hideously grotesque in the black cloth hood over his head with mere slits for eyes and mouth, and the long black robe he wore down to his ankles like a woman's gown.

One gets accustomed to anything in time, and Alison knew by now that he was just another greedy criminal using her to extort money from her father. She was a brave little girl, and already her fear was giving way to anger and icy contempt. She had already deduced from his voice, despite its tone of menace, that he was a young man, probably only a few years older than herself, and he didn't speak in the idiom of an ill-educated lout.

'Why are you hiding behind that mask?' she said. 'Is it some silly game you're playing?'

'It's for your own protection,' he replied. 'If you see my face you'll never get out of here alive, even if your father does pay up. You can understand that, can't you?'

'I see,' she replied, feeling her blood curdle at the cold, calm, factual statement. But she continued to stare at his eyes which were dark and intimidating, and she knew she would always remember them whether he wore a hood or not.

'You want to go back to your parents, don't you?'

'Yes, of course I do.'

'Well, just behave yourself and you might make it. Don't try to be clever and find out things not good for you to know. Above all, don't try running away, because you won't get ten yards past the door. The guard dog you heard is a killer. He's always loose to patrol the grounds, and he'll pull you down and tear your throat out if he catches you in the open. Listen.'

In the silence she suddenly heard the snuffling of the dog's breath and a low eager whine as he sniffed on the other side of the closed door.

'How long are you going to keep me here?' she asked.

'A few days without communication to get your father into a paying-up disposition. If he pays promptly when asked, without any tricks or conspiracies with the police, you should be free inside a week or ten days. If he won't pay, he won't get you back. That's all. Work it out where you'll be.'

Alison felt her despair intensify.

'Am I supposed to sleep on that filthy thing?' she said, indicating an old stained mattress on the floor that looked positively verminous.

'Why not?' he replied curtly. 'The dog's slept on it.'

'But I'm cold.'

'There's a couple of blankets. What more d'you want?'

'They look as if the dog's slept on them too.'

'Tough luck,' he replied brutally. 'If you

were tied hand and foot with a dog's
collar and chain round your neck, you'd
have something to moan about. I know
this humble accommodation is not quite
what you're used to. But then you're a
highly privileged little girl. That's why
you're here.'

She looked despairingly round her
prison, which was about twenty feet
square. The massive oak beams which
supported the roof were a few feet above
her, and over them the naked rafters
draped with a century's cobwebs. Up one
corner on the dusty floorboards was a pile
of old sacks in which bran and oats for
the horses had once been kept. There was
a small window high up in one wall, and a
single item of furniture, an old mahogany
upright chair whose cane seat had a large
hole in it. In the dim light of the oil lamp
the pitiless squalor of the prison was
sinister and over-powering.

'What about the lavatory?' she said. 'It
must have occurred to you that I'm going
to need one.'

'I'll get you a bucket to put under that
hole in the chair,' he said. 'That's what

State prisoners have to use, and on that level you're no better than they are.'

He picked up the hurricane lamp and moved towards the door.

'Oh, please leave me the lamp,' she pleaded. 'I hate being completely in the dark.'

'What! Leave fire and paraffin in the hands of a hysterical little girl!' he scoffed. 'An open invitation to bring the fire brigade here. Curl up on your luxury divan and forget it.'

'Don't I get anything to drink?'

'You won't die of thirst and malnutrition between now and morning. D'you think this is the Ritz?'

Alison heard him fix a padlock on the outside of the stout oak door and mutter something to whoever was there holding the dog on a leash. She heard receding footsteps over the floorboards, and the snuffling ceased as the dog went with them. Half an hour later she heard the roar of a motor bike starting up and roaring away till its exhaust note vanished in the distance. One of them at least had gone, but the dog would still be on the premises.

All she could hear now was the sighing of the autumn wind in the nearby trees, and the faint rustling of what she thought must be vermin in the pile of provision sacks. She was so cold by now that even the blankets which smelt strongly of the dog were acceptable to wrap herself in. As she lay shivering in the total blackness, the harsh reality of her predicament really got to her. She wept with fear for the future and self-pity that she should have been singled out for this appalling treatment. She thought of her mother, still blissfully asleep in the house and unaware of what had happened. How was she going to take it in the morning when she discovered her only child was missing?

Alison had had a row with her mother only last evening because Alison wanted a pair of high-heeled platform shoes that all the other girls wore at school. But Mrs. Norman insisted in her square, old-fashioned way that such footwear was ridiculous and unstable and would cause damage to spine and pelvis by holding her feet at that absurdly steep angle. Alison always lost when her mother pronounced what was best for her. She was fussy and over-protective at the best of times. This calamity would drive her insane.

Alison knew that her father could be relied on to raise hell in every quarter, spurring on the police to turn the world upside down. But she knew realistically that their chances of finding her in this remote and distant prison were almost nil. Her only hope of life was that her father would hand over the money the kidnappers wanted without anything going wrong, and that the criminals would then keep faith.

She hardly slept at all through the cold and fear, and at last came a time when a square of grey light began to show on the darkened window. Soon it was full daylight and all the contours of her prison were picked out in the gloomy half-light that filtered through the dirty glass. She climbed stiffly to her feet and started running round the room to get warm.

Two hours later she heard footsteps and the dog's heavy breathing outside. The door was unlocked and a man came in with her breakfast on a tray. The dog came padding in behind him, held on a chain. It was a huge black beast with a brindled snout and tawny belly, a square head and massive jaws and pointed ears. He fixed Alison with his yellow feral eyes, lifted a lip to display a hideous array of fangs, and growled deep in his throat as if warning her what to expect if she ran for it. But he remained quiescent under the authority of his handler and made no attempt to attack. Although she'd been brought up for many years with a dog in the house, and had learnt to like and trust dogs, Alison instinctively shrank from the bristling ferocity of this beast.

The man was small, dark and wiry, with lank black hair under his cloth cap, and small black eyes with a singular lack of expression. He had a pointed, weaselly face, thin lips and a sallow, unhealthy looking skin. He was dressed in dirty old corduroy trousers, rubber gum boots and an old tweed jacket several sizes too large for him, like a farm labourer. His age could have been anything between thirty and fifty.

Alison wondered why he had made no attempt to mask his face as her other captor had done. He put the tray down on the floor beside her mattress and then stood watching her expectantly. The dog sat down and did likewise.

'Is this supposed to be my breakfast?' said Alison.

'Ar, tha's right,' he grunted.

She lifted the cover off one dish and found it contained scrambled egg. In the other was a breakfast cereal with milk. Finally there was a pot of watery coffee.

'Are you sure you can spare all this?' said Alison who'd regained some of her courage from this workaday situation and the squalid ordinariness of this insignificant menial.

'Ar,' he replied.

'You can go away now then,' she said disdainfully. 'I'm not likely to use the crockery to make my escape with.'

'You'm to eat it fust. Then I takes it,' he said doggedly in his southern regional dialect.

'Oh, all right,' she replied sulkily.

Having recovered her normally healthy

appetite, she set to work and demolished all the food in two minutes flat, while the dog and the man looked on impassively.

'Are you one of the gang?' said Alison conversationally. 'How much money are you hoping to get out of me?'

The labourer stared at her vacantly, and suddenly Alison realised the truth about him. He was retarded, or in more straightforward terms, a half-wit, a cretin, who probably didn't even understand the concept of kidnapping and extortion. This must be why his masters didn't bother to make him hide his face from her. He'd just been ordered to feed her and keep her there like some pet animal, ensuring above all that she did not escape. His was not to reason why. But she had no doubt at all he would automatically send the dog to pull her down if she tried to run for it. Obviously one of his few skills was dog-handling.

'What's your name?' she said with a friendly smile.

'Arold.'

'And what's your doggie's name?'

'Oh, he be Rufus.'

'Hullo Rufus,' she said conciliatingly.

But the black dog merely raised his supercilious lip again and rumbled menacingly, incorruptible against all offers of friendship.

'Do you know why I'm being kept here, Harold?'

Still the impassive vacant stare.

'I'm being held prisoner here,' said Alison. 'It's against the law. So the police will come and put you in prison for keeping me here against my will. Do you know the police, Harold?'

For the first time his eyes seemed to flicker with light and life.

'Oh ar. I knows um. Daft lot o' buggers they be.'

'But if you were to let me go, Harold, everybody would be your friend. You wouldn't go to prison with the others. My father would give you money for helping me.'

'Arrgh, lot o' bloody nonsense,' he growled. 'You'm finished then?'

'Yes, thank you, Harold.'

He shuffled forward, picked up the tray and carried it out, carefully locking the door behind him.

Left alone, Alison felt dispirited by the encounter. The vague general strategy she'd just formulated of getting through to the cretinous Harold and seducing him from his criminal allegiance was going to be uphill work.

All that morning she was left completely alone in her prison so that she felt demoralised with the boredom and suspense. She examined the door, but it was built of old-fashioned stout oak planks, and even if she broke it down she still had the dog to contend with. She lifted the broken cane chair on to the pile of sacks, and by standing precariously on the rim of the chair she was able to reach the window. It didn't open, but by wiping the encrusted dirt away from the panes she was able at last to see through it to the environment of her prison.

There were big stately old trees with their yellowing foliage, vast rolling acres of seemingly empty parkland and a long driveway disappearing into the desolate countryside that Alison distrusted. Close by was the jutting wing of a big old house built of grey stone. As she looked down she saw a stooping, frail old man dressed in a brown felt hat and belted overcoat walk slowly into view from the house with the aid of a walking stick.

It was unthinkable that a man so old and debilitated could be one of the criminals, or even be aware of what was going on at the house. So she hammered on the window and screamed at the top of her voice to attract his attention. But the old man tottered infirmly on his way down the drive without turning round. Probably he was senile and devoid of all his faculties.

Nothing else happened all morning. At midday Harold came again with his dog on a chain, carrying a tray of minced meat and spaghetti, with stewed apples and custard for the second course.

'Is this all there is?' said Alison, turning up her nose with disgust.

'Ar, that's her,' said Harold.

'Well, I can't stand mince and I hate spaghetti. I've had custard with everything at school till I'm practically the same colour. Give my compliments to the chef, and tell him he should be in another job.'

'Ar,' said Harold gravely, standing there and looking at her.

'I'm not going to eat it,' said Alison. 'I'd rather starve. You may as well take it away.'

The menial stood there with his dog for a quarter of an hour watching her, while Alison sat stubbornly on her mattress with her back to him, and the food congealed to an inedible greasy mess. At last Harold got the message, picked up the unused tray and wandered out again with the dog.

The interminable afternoon dragged on with Alison pacing round her prison, watching the habits of spiders, woodlice and other wild life to alleviate the boredom. At about six o'clock came the faithful dog-handler with another tray of food. This consisted of a boiled egg, some thick wedges of bread and butter and a pot of tea. Having disposed of it, she asked Harold to tell his masters she needed more bedding to keep her warm, a light to see by and a transistor radio. He said 'Ar' indifferently and wandered off. Her request had fallen on deaf ears.

She settled down with growing depression to another night of total darkness and cramping cold in the inadequate bedding. The days passed in boredom and despair and she was becoming disorientated about the passage of time. Three days in that prison seemed like a month.

On the night of the fifth day of her solitary confinement, when Alison was in a fitful doze, she was awakened by the man in the black robe and hood who seemed only to operate in the small hours. Alison felt a pang of fear which she tried to smother beneath her contempt for him. But at least he was a stimulating change of scenery from the moronic Harold.

Her captor tossed her a bundle of clothes, consisting of an old red woollen sweater, a pair of woman's trousers and a man's brown overcoat similar to the one she'd seen on the frail old man walking down the drive. All the garments were old and well worn, and wouldn't have been accepted in a jumble sale.

'Wear these,' he said. 'I want your own coat.'

'What for?'

'Just to prove to your old man that we really possess the right parcel. Like any good bourgeois, he wants to be sure what he's buying before he tips up his bread. I'll have a piece of your hair as well, just to clinch it.'

He took a large pair of tailor's scissors from under his robe and snipped off a lock of her long dark hair.

She felt like weeping and pleading with him to let her out of this dirty, dilapidated rat-hole. She wanted a clean comfortable bed and warmth inside a house, with bathing facilities to clean herself up, to look at a book, listen to a radio and re-establish contact with the civilised world. But her spirit was unbroken, and she wouldn't give this creep the satisfaction of seeing her distress.

'How much longer are you going to keep me here?' she demanded.

'There's no hurry,' he replied casually. 'Everything's proceeding according to plan. Collecting the ransom is a job that has to be carefully planned. It can't be rushed.'

'Do you really think you're going to get away with this?' she said. 'The last man who tried it on in this country got thirty years.'

'Well, if that happens to me, you won't be around to rejoice,' he replied brutally. 'The penalty for murder in this absurd country is no heavier than that for kidnapping. So you can be damned sure I'll dispose of the evidence if things look like going wrong.'

Alison thought this over and her heart sank at its brutal logic.

'Your partner in crime is a woman, isn't she?' said Alison.

He glowered at her malevolently from under his hood.

'I've warned you about being too clever for your own good, haven't I?'

'I didn't have to be clever to work that out. She drove the van on the night I was brought here. I smelt her perfume, and these old trousers and sweater belong to her. How do petty crooks like you come to have the run of a country house? Or have you taken someone else prisoner?'

'Shut up,' he snarled. 'You're in no position to ask questions. If you get away from here with your life, it's as much as you can expect.'

'Why doesn't your woman friend come to see me for some girl talk?' persisted Alison. 'She should know how important it is to me to have a bath and clean my teeth. Besides, if I'm to be kept here much longer I'm going to need some of the things women need. She ought to know that, unless she's as stupid as your dogsbody and his dog.'

'What makes you think anybody gives a damn about your sordid little animal needs?' he replied. 'You can bleed, you little bitch, for all anybody cares. You're nothing, just a pawn, a bargaining counter, practically dead already. Just start praying that the ransom pick-up goes off successfully.

He stalked out with her overcoat and lock of hair, and locked the door behind him. Alison sank down on her smelly mattress and wept with absolute despair.

6

Unknown to the police, Donald Norman had received his instructions about the money from the kidnappers.

A fourteen-year-old youth, playing truant from school, was accosted by a woman who stopped alongside him in a taxi about fifty yards from the main entrance of Norman Plastics in New Cross. She wore dark glasses and a wide-brimmed hat with a black veil, so that the boy saw very little of her face. But he knew she was as good-looking as a film star, and her perfume positively gushed out through the open taxi window at him. Some tart!

She asked him in a top-drawer accent if he wanted to earn a pound. He said, 'You betcha, ma'am!' So she gave him a plain manila envelope addressed to Donald Norman.

'Go hand this to that man in uniform standing at the factory gate,' she said.

'Then come back here and collect your pound.'

So the flustered youth rushed off on his bike and handed in the note to the red-necked security man on the gate, while the taxi waited with its engine ticking over. The woman watched him closely, and when he came back with mission accomplished, she handed over a pound note without a word. She tapped the stolid driver on the shoulder like a duchess, and the taxi drove away. The youth sat astride his bike, staring after it in perplexity, reflecting that it was the easiest and nicest quid he'd ever earned in his life. Better than mugging or dipping.

Up in his private office, trembling with guilty dread, Norman tore open the envelope which had just been delivered by internal runner, and extracted a flimsy piece of paper with a typewritten message.

'Arrange withdrawal of £75,000 in cash (used one-pound notes) when your cashiers collect the weekly payroll for your workers tomorrow. A confidential note to your bank manager should do the trick. If he turns awkward and won't divi up, it's good night to Alison. Likewise if any copper sticks his nose in, or there's any attempt at a double-cross, or the money isn't all there. The police have got to be kept right out if you ever want to see the girl alive again. Put the money in a suitcase and come alone by hired car to the crossroads a mile south of Sutton on the A217. On the right, just past a bus stop is a phone box. Arrange to be there at ten o'clock tomorrow night, no earlier and no later. Instructions on where to deliver the suitcase will be taped underneath the telephone pay box. This is absolutely your last and only chance. Cross me up or bring in the fuzz, and I swear that I'll give you back your daughter a piece at a time.'

After reading this, Donald Norman was in such a state of panic terror that it took two large whiskies to steady his nerves. It never occurred to him to do anything else but obey the kidnapper implicitly and keep the message absolutely secret. He never even dared to tell his wife of the new development. The brutal tone and implications of the letter had established complete psychological dominance over him. Nothing else was real or valid except that gruesome threat to Alison. In Norman's present state of mind the police existed for him merely as a potential menace that could get Alison killed. He picked up his telephone and rang the crime squad's H.Q. in Bermondsey, asking for Detective Sergeant Scamp.

'I want your assurance that when the kidnapper approaches me about the ransom, you'll hold off and leave me free to negotiate Alison's release,' said Norman.

'Why?' demanded Scamp sharply. 'Have you been contacted?'

'No,' lied Norman. 'But I expect I shall be soon, and I don't want to put Alison's life at risk by having you lot crashing about trying to arrest the kidnapper at a delicate moment. So I'm asking you as a special favour to call your men off while we make the transaction.'

'Do you realise what you're asking?' said Scamp incredulously. 'Do you think you can deal with these people on a straightforward man-to-man basis? You could get yourself killed, have Alison killed, and still make them a present of the money.'

'Do you think I care about the money, or my own life as long as there's some chance of getting Alison back alive?' cried Norman hysterically. 'One sure way to get her killed is to have you lot spring a trap that misfires, leaving Alison in the kidnappers' hands for them to take their revenge on.'

'I understand your concern, Mr. Norman,' said Scamp, 'but it doesn't lie in my power to make the police back off from a criminal case once they've got their teeth into it. I'll take your request to my superiors, but I don't for one moment think they'll agree.'

'Not even to save Alison's life?' shrieked Norman distraught. 'What sort of idiots are you?'

'We don't agree that total capitulation to these people is the best way to save her life.'

'But it's been proved in Italy, where

there's someone from a wealthy family kidnapped nearly every week. As long as the relatives pay the asking price and the police discreetly look the other way without trying to capture the kidnappers, the hostage is invariably returned unharmed.'

'I know,' retorted Scamp, 'and that's why kidnapping has become the only growth industry in that country. If we compound a felony by abdicating from your case, and kidnapping here is seen to be a soft touch, how long before dozens of other fathers are going through what you're enduring now?'

'Screw all the other!' yelled Norman frenziedly. 'What do I care about them as long as I get Alison back?'

'I'm sorry you feel like that,' said Scamp smoothly. 'In your own interests and Alison's interests we're still relying on you to let us know as soon as you're approached by the kidnappers.'

'All right then,' raved Norman, foaming at the mouth. 'All right. But I shall hold you responsible if anything happens to Alison.'

'We won't let you down,' Scamp

reassured him. 'Don't forget. Instant information to us as soon as you get a message about time and place.'

Donald Norman slammed the phone down with an oath of execration about flat-footed coppers.

Scamp, not liking the sound of things, wrote out a report on Norman's request and probable state of mind, adding as his opinion that things might soon be moving in the Dulwich kidnapping affair. He recommended that detectives on surveillance at Norman's house should now be particularly watchful in case the industrialist tried to effect a rendezvous on his own with the kidnappers.

The following evening he was proved right. At about eight o'clock there came an excited radio call from D. C. Huddlestone, on watch outside the Normans' house in Dulwich.

'There's somebody just delivered a car to Norman's house,' he said. 'Ford Granada. Looks like a Hertz hire car. The driver's handed in the keys to Norman, and gone away on foot. The car's standing in the drive.'

Scamp was on night duty with the stand-by squad, and he knew immediately that the balloon was going up. Something nasty was about to happen, and he didn't want to be caught master-minding the coming operation, which could bring down more brickbats than glory on his head.

He rang up Detective Inspector Earwacker who was off duty at home in the suburbs, watching television, and pitched it in his lap.

'All right,' grumbled Earwacker resignedly. 'Trust the buggers to screw up my Friday night's viewing. A Hertz hire car, you say? He must be going to make the drop. He's ratted on us, the stupid bastard. Tell Huddlestone to follow him when he moves off, but not to get too close in case Norman susses him. I'm going straight over there to join with the other mobiles. Keep me informed of your position, which direction Norman's heading, and give me details of the hire car. With any luck we'll be able to pick him up along the route, keep him boxed in without him knowing, and jump them all at the pick-up point.'

'Let's hope it works out that way, guv,' said Scamp.

He took a radio-equipped C.I.D. car from the motor pool, and set off for Dulwich. As he reached Brockwell Park, D. C. Huddlestone came on the air with another message.

'Norman's leaving the house with a big suitcase, looking all round him like a burglar. He's getting in the hire car as if he'd nicked it. He's off now . . . Seems to be heading for Gallery Road. He's not pushing it at all. Speed is about thirty-five m.p.h . . .

'Now he's going south, seems to be heading for Upper Norwood.'

A few minutes later Detective Inspector Earwacker came on the air from the command vehicle with Scamp's call sign:

'Daisy Foxtrot, what's your position? Over.'

'I'm on the A204 heading for Tulse Hill,' said Scamp.

'Change to the A205 at Tulse Hill, and then continue south on the A23. I reckon he's heading for the sticks, so we'll close with him on a parallel course.'

Presently D. C. Huddlestone came on and said:

'He's made a sharp right at Broad Green and is now heading west. I reckon his present route will take him well north of Croydon and into Sutton.'

'Stay with him,' said Earwacker.

Shortly afterwards Scamp reported: 'I'm now on the A297 direct route into Sutton, and I estimate I should be there just before him.'

'Good,' said Earwacker. 'Wait at the traffic lights in Sutton, and pick him up on the intersection.'

Within less than three minutes Scamp spotted the dark green Ford Granada described by D. C. Huddlestone, and verified its registration number as the car hired by Norman. It was stopped at the traffic lights, but when they changed to green Norman's car turned left past the church and started heading south on the A297 at the usual comfortable speed.

Scamp, momentarily trapped by the red light, informed the other cars of the change of direction. D. C. Huddlestone increased his speed to keep Norman in view. Two miles further south Scamp had caught up with them, and suddenly noticed that they were slowing down. Huddlestone stopped on the grass verge where the road ran past a golf course, and Scamp pulled in behind him.

'Has he stopped yet?' said Scamp.

'Yes, skipper. At that telephone kiosk by the crossroads. Can you see it? Looks as if he's waiting in the car. No, he's off again. Here we go.'

Norman had located the telephone box, but it was still only ten minutes to ten and he'd been told to go there at ten o'clock exactly. Determined to obey instructions to the letter and not offend the criminals, he decided to cruise round for ten minutes, and headed south again.

Scamp forged ahead and overtook him, so that Norman was now boxed in by the two police cars. Two miles further south, looking in his mirror, Scamp saw the hire car turn off left into a minor road. Immediately he did a U-turn and went back to locate him, instructing Huddlestone to follow.

Norman went round the dark lanes in a narrow loop and rejoined the main road a few hundred yards north of where he'd left it. Then he jogged on comfortably to arrive back at the kiosk close on the stroke of ten.

'He must be waiting for a phone call at a given time,' said Scamp, watching through his night intensive glasses as Norman got out of his car and went across the road to the phone box. 'No, he's not phoning. He's groping under the coin box.'

Norman quickly found the strip of paper taped to the metal under-surface. It said: 'Travel south on this road. Take the right fork, B 2032, to Pebble Coombe. Turn sharp right and then left on unclassified road crossing Headley Heath. Stop at small church on the right. Wait in car for contact.'

The detectives watched Norman turn his car round carefully as the traffic permitted, and come back towards them. When he'd gone past, they too turned round and followed him, a hundred yards between vehicles.

Shortly afterwards, with a maniacal roar, a motor bike overtook them going flat out, with a black figure hunched over the handlebars, and disappeared into the distance, the beam of the headlight cutting like a lance through the misty autumn night. It looked as if Norman was under surveillance by the kidnapper, and the implications filled Scamp with renewed foreboding.

He called up and reported the fact to Earwacker, who was still a few miles away coming down through Morden.

'Couldn't you have stopped him or run him off the road?' said Earwacker peevishly.

'At the rate he was going I could only have stopped him by killing him,' rejoined Scamp, 'and then we'd never find out where Alison is being kept. Besides, it could just have been a harmless punk rocker out for a burn-up. D'you want me on a manslaughter charge?'

'Over and out,' snarled Earwacker.

On the B road with less traffic about in the dark countryside, it was more tricky to keep Norman in view without betraying their presence and intent. They could only manage it by the hazardous and unlawful technique of travelling without lights. At Pebble Coombe, where the road turned sharply in two right-angled bends, they lost him, suddenly blinded by the glare of two oncoming vehicles which momentarily drowned out the glow of Norman's headlights. Scamp was worried when they came to a fork in the road, either of which could have been taken by the quarry, so he let Huddle-stone continue along the main road, while he took the left fork along the narrow lane over the heath. He informed Earwacker of what had happened and the other mobiles were ordered to converge on the two roads.

Meanwhile the terrified and distraught father, acting for the best according to his lights, had stopped beside the small isolated church. He sat in his stationary car in the middle of the lane with his headlights full on and his engine still running, the cold sweat of fear trickling down his backbone. In the ghostly countryside with thick forest on one side and open heathland on the other, the squat little Saxon church looked more like a place for Satanic devilry at midnight than a shrine of Christian worship.

Norman now began to have agonised, panic-stricken doubts as to whether he'd done the right thing in disobeying the police and coming out to this lonely place with seventy-five thousand pounds and no protection to meet a ruthless criminal. What guarantee did he have, if he handed over the money, that Alison would be given back safe and sound? How did he really know she was still alive? What if he himself was the target of some old, forgotten enemy, and Alison was only the bait to lure him out here where he could be robbed and killed.

Scamp came carefully round a corner, groping his way in the dark. He saw the glow of stationary lights up ahead and realised he'd found his quarry at the rendezvous. He coasted quietly to a standstill two hundred yards away, verified with his night glasses that it was really Norman's hire car, and picked up the radio transmitter.

'Daisy Foxtrot to X-ray. I think I'm at the pick-up point. Quarry is stopped up ahead by the old church on Headley Heath. I suggest all mobiles converge on this Map Reference at top speed.'

He gave the six-figure Map Reference on his Ordnance Survey map, and Earwacker issued instructions to the other vehicles to move on a course enabling them to intercept anybody travelling along the lonely road where Scamp suspected that Norman was about to meet the kidnapper.

Meanwhile the black-clad motor cyclist had been sitting up in the woods opposite the church, astride his silent motor bike, with his eyes fixed on Norman's lit-up car. He waited some minutes to be sure that Norman had not been followed. Then he came coasting silently down the bridlepath through the woods to collect his jackpot.

Neither he nor Scamp nor Donald Norman knew that there were other eyes fixed on this eerie scene.

Drawn up off the road and hidden

118

cosily under the trees near the church, a local farmer's wife, bored, discontented, on the verge of middle age, was having it off in the back of her car with a personable young plumber whom she'd taken a fancy to when he came to fix her central heating. As she'd got a suspicious and boorish husband with a drinking problem and a violent temper, the two lovers cowered down petrified with fear at the sight of the car unaccountably stopped in the road with its headlights full on. They thought it was the husband who'd trailed them to their trysting place and was playing cat and mouse with them before he made the expected onslaught with his circus-trainer's whip.

Suddenly in the dimly reflected glow from Norman's lights among the trees, the lovers saw the evil black figure astride his motor bike coasting silently towards them down the bridlepath. Their obsessive guilt convinced them that they were under attack, that the brutal husband had hired some Hell's Angels to give them the traditional beating.

Desperately the plumber leaned over

the front seat and switched the headlights full on. Still minus his trousers, he vaulted into the driver's seat and started up for a racing getaway.

Shocked and startled beyond belief by the brilliant lights blasting at him out of the trees, the motor cyclist immediately concluded he was in a police ambush, that somehow Norman had tricked him. Frantically he started the bike, kicked it into gear and shot out of the woods in a cloud of dust and stones, roaring away south west in the direction away from Scamp.

Realising from the sudden appearance of car lights and the roar of the motor bike that everything had gone wrong, Scamp grabbed his radio microphone.

'Operation aborted,' he said. 'Stand by to stop motor cyclist heading south west from last given map reference towards Leatherhead.'

He started his engine and drove forward rapidly in pursuit. Norman was still sitting in his car, frozen with fear, aware that disaster had struck, yet unable to evaluate otherwise the sudden out-break of wild activity all round him.

Scamp managed to squeeze past Norman's car by mounting the grass verge and ploughing through some brushwood at the edge of the trees. But the car containing the plumber and his mate was already out of the woods just ahead of him, swaying recklessly in the same direction as the motor cyclist.

In a few minutes Scamp encountered the other police vehicles who'd intercepted and stopped the lovers' car. But none of them had seen the motor cyclist. He must have dodged into some field or wood to elude them, for he evidently had a first-class knowledge of the terrain.

Detective Inspector Earwacker was raging with furious despair at this monumental cock-up with its possible repercussions on his career and the unpredictable dangers for the kidnapped victim. He sent the cars to comb all the roads and lanes converging on the A25 from Leatherhead to Dorking, but though they were zooming round for more than an hour, they didn't see a single black-clad motor cyclist.

'A bad business, guv,' said Scamp as

they stopped at the roadside for a rapid conference. 'If only those idiots hadn't startled him when they did, we'd have had him cold getting the money off Norman. I suppose we'd better go back and have it out with Norman. He's going to blame us for this mess.'

'I'm pissed off with Norman,' raged Earwacker. 'I've got no sympathy for him at all. What with him going it alone, not telling us a thing, and then a couple of motorised snoggers choosing the actual meeting point to do their thing, it couldn't have been a bigger mess.'

'One thing I'm sure of now, guv, we're dealing with amateurs. The whole thing reeks of a botch-up from start to finish, and that's why it's so dangerous for the girl. What worries me now is how the kidnapper will react in the next hour or two. He has to be a psychopath and a nutter, or he wouldn't have snatched Alison in the first place. So what'll he do to Alison when he finds he's been cheated out of the money through running into a police stake-out? If he thinks there's no hope of collecting the ransom safely, he could kill the girl through sheer malice, and we'll never hear from him again.'

'Do you have any more cheering suggestions?' said Earwacker morosely, thinking of the cold fury of the Assistant Commissioner (Crime), and the Home Office's devious ways of hastening Earwacker's retirement. 'If Norman reveals this shambles to the newspapers, we're all going to be fried in the full blaze of the gutter.'

7

The motor cyclist, realising that he'd walked into a well co-ordinated police ambush, rode recklessly without lights and shot off the metalled road as soon as he saw other approaching headlights glaring over the trees up ahead. He roared off down a rutted track to an isolated farm, opened the gate into the farmyard, drove through it and up the hill on the other side. He rode across a grass field, standing up on the foot-rests like a scrambler, as he hit holes and tussocks which nearly threw him off. He crossed a couple of stubble fields and emerged on a sandy footpath alongside a wood. He followed this down to a five-barred gate which opened on to a bridlepath.

In the distance he could see the lights of cars moving fast along a road, which his knowledge of the countryside told him was the road to Leatherhead. But he knew police patrol cars, summoned by radio, would be patrolling all the major and minor roads over a wide area, looking for a solitary motor cyclist in black.

So he crossed the main road when the traffic permitted, plunged across a golf course, coming off several times as he hit the bunkers, and continued across open farmland in a wide circle north of Leatherhead. He had to use the main road for a mile to cross the railway line and the River Rye. But his luck held, and there were no police cars to challenge him. As soon as possible he left the road and turned off across Leatherhead Common.

Three quarters of an hour later he roared up the treelined drive of the old manor house where Alison was kept prisoner.

The terror and excitement of the chase had given him a strange and savage stimulation which was heightened by the vicious anger he felt at being double-crossed by Norman. They'd treated him like a fool when he had the power of life or death over the girl. So much the worse for all of them. It would serve old

Norman right if he returned her dead body to the house in Dulwich an arm and leg at a time. Maybe he'd do that in the end, but not before he'd had his own kind of sport with the little bitch. With him all viciousness craved a sexual outlet.

Alison was dozing fitfully and unhappily under her dog blankets when he unlocked the door and crashed into her prison carrying the usual hurricane lamp.

Alison started up fearfully, for she could tell by the erupting violence of his entry that he was frenzied with rage and meant her no good. The anger radiated from behind his black mask.

'Your fool of a father double-crossed me,' he raged. 'He told the police and they had an ambush waiting. He values his blasted money more than you. I warned him what would happen if he tried it on. I told him he'd never see you alive again. So you'd better start saying your prayers.'

'Oh no,' she gasped, frightened by his cold fury. 'Don't come near me. You'll never get away with it if you hurt me. The police — '

'The police!' he snarled contemptuously. 'Those thickheads couldn't catch a cold. I don't know whether to feed you to the dog, or keep you alive a bit longer and give your old man a second chance to buy your life. Maybe it would convince him we're not fooling if I send him one of your ears.'

As he stared down at her cowering form, such a thin, frail, colourless little thing, her unformed childishness and essential innocence as well as her shrinking horror thrilled him with the cruel ecstasy he knew so well. Already he had an erection.

'Take your clothes off,' he commanded.

'No,' she sobbed. 'Oh no! I won't.'

'Get them off, down to the last stitch.'

'No.'

'If I have to do it for you, you'll lose a few teeth in the process.'

Knowing she had no choice, trembling with horror, she stripped off all her clothes. As he advanced on her, unbuttoning the front of his black robe to expose himself, she suddenly had a shocked realisation that he was wearing the garb of a priest, a worsted cassock.

She endured his savage assault and nothing was spared her. She screamed with the pain, the terror, the degradation, hoping for only one thing, that he'd finish it off by strangling her.

He withdrew from her with animals grunts of satisfaction, picked up his lantern without a word, and went out, locking the door behind him, leaving her a quivering hysterical wreck. Henceforth she would see in all men the grotesque, priest-like figure who'd murdered her innocence.

There was nobody to comfort or heal or console her, nothing but the cold clinging darkness in which she was cocooned. She sobbed for hours until she fell asleep from the exhaustion of suffering.

When she awoke in the morning to the shameful humiliation that would never be washed away, she was resolved to kill herself, for she understood at last why they called rape a fate worse than death. One leg of her trousers tied round a beam, the other in a slip-knot round her neck, and the broken mahogany chair to jump from should ensure her death.

Before she could arrange it, however, she heard a fumbling at the lock outside, and Harold came in with the breakfast tray, the dog slavering menacingly at his heels.

'Ar,' said Harold, as Alison hurriedly wrapped herself in a blanket and turned her tear-stained face away. 'Ar, you'm upset then.'

In her present distraught state she hadn't noticed the near miracle of the half-witted menial recording an observation and making a comment, but she saw its significance when she thought about it later. She couldn't eat the usual scrambled eggs, but she drank the hot coffee thankfully, and felt slightly better after it.

As the scruffy little man stood there watching her with his moronic interest in her condition, Alison's shame, defeat and despair slowly curdled to hatred. Who did these scum think they were, even to imagine they could get away with these multiple outrages? Somebody was going to pay for all this. Even though she hated her life, she'd hang on to it long enough to stand up in court and point the finger at these subhuman animals who'd locked her up and maltreated her. She didn't care about anything any more now that she'd been defiled by that hideous act of raw butchery. She had nothing to lose. Maybe even the cretinous Harold would start getting ideas along those lines, and if he did, Alison suddenly had a desperate idea how she could exploit the situation to make her escape. She had brains and Harold was a moron, so Harold must be the weak link in the criminals' chain, and she was going through with it whatever happened. They'd delegated responsibility to Harold beyond his capabilities, and it would cost them all they had. That damned dog wasn't going to stop her either. She would never have dreamt of such a scheme or had the will to try it out if she hadn't lost her finer sensibilities through being raped.

'Harold,' she said coaxingly, 'I need a bowl of hot water, some soap and a towel. Will you be an angel and get them for me? I'll be nice to you, Harold. I really like you. I'll be your friend in the nicest way.'

Nonchalantly she let the shielding blanket fall away and revealed a generous expanse of her slim white thigh. A spark of excited interest gleamed in Harold's dull eyes, and for the first time she realised that she'd got through to him. Obviously sex was the lever by which you could move even Harold. He went out with alacrity and came back shortly afterwards with an old aluminium bowl of hot water, some carbolic soap and a kitchen towel taken from a roller on the door.

8

Within two days of the word going out on him, there was news of Jack Hansler from that evergreen source of information on human derelicts, the Department of Health and Social Security. News came from the police station at Epsom in Surrey that Hansler was living there on Social Security, a long-standing member of the hard-core unemployed. He was in lodgings with a poor family called Cowie in a first-floor flat in a run-down Victorian apartment house which, ironically, was next door to one of Epsom's branch banks.

The local police had had no trouble from Hansler since he'd been there. He was a spent force, a poor down-at-heel bum who'd paid his debts to Society and come out a loser, too beaten down to nick a milk bottle from a doorstep or kite a cheque. The local C.I.D. were frankly surprised that he was wanted for questioning in the Alison Norman kidnapping case.

Scamp drove down to Epsom accompanied by D. C. Burgess, and knocked on the door of Hansler's address. They were greeted by a poor-looking woman, pale, jaded and overworked, with her unkempt hair bedraggled like so many rats' tails, and three or four toddlers clutching at her skirts.

'Mr. Hansler?' she said fearfully. 'What you want him for?'

Scamp introduced himself and Mrs. Cowie looked even more scared.

'He's out walkin' his dog,' she said. 'You'll find him in the park, or sittin' on a seat by the bus stop, or in the churchyard. He'll be back for his dinner though.'

'Good, we'll wait for him here,' said Scamp, 'if you don't mind us coming in.'

The woman showed them into her living-room, which was cluttered with children's toys and bulky, worn-out furniture. It smelt of wet clothes, old dust, stale cooking and poverty. The woman's husband was also out of work and they could hear him crashing about in the kitchen, blaspheming freely as he tried to make a pigeons' cage out of knocked-off materials.

After about half an hour the front door opened and Helen Webster's former husband came in, faithfully accompanied by a black, slobbering, tail-wagging old mongrel. Hansler was in his fifties, a pale-faced, watery-eyed, stoop-shouldered man, dressed in a shabby raincoat, old-fashioned baggy trousers and down-at-heel shoes. He hadn't washed or shaved that morning, and he had an undernourished, debilitated look. He'd been on the skids so long that decrepit listlessness was built into him. Normally diffident and nervous, the ex-swindler was always scared out of his wits by strangers seeking him out, for in his lifelong experience the unknown could only mean trouble.

He recoiled in sheer panic at the knowledge that these were detectives from the Met. Long after expiation his guilt had never left him.

'Why me, guvnor? I'm clean,' he protested with the recidivist's plaintive whine. 'My last rap was five years ago, and everything was taken into consideration.'

'It's about your wife, Mr. Hansler,' said Scamp.

'Yeah, I know. She's dead. Mr. Pyke from the local nick told me,' said Hansler dejectedly. 'I'm sorry and all that, but she's not my business. I've not seen her for twelve or thirteen years. She wasn't a bad sort, as women go. But you know something, guv. I can't even remember what she looked like.'

He shuffled out of his sleazy raincoat, sat down at the table and started making a cigarette from old dog-ends in a tin, rolling the paper cylinder expertly in his long, sensitive fingers, with the slow, deft precision of long years in penal solitude.

'You've not really come to see me about Helen,' he said, having thought it out, 'not big-time crime busters like you. She never nicked a thing in her life, and you know my slate's clean. So what's going on, guv?'

'You once worked for Mr. Norman of Norman Plastics in New Cross,' said Scamp. 'It was while working for him that you got your biggest bust, five years for theft and embezzlement.'

'So?' muttered Hansler, looking shifty.

'So your wife went to work for Norman as his housekeeper just after you went down, and stayed there a good many years. One way and another you could both be said to be somewhat heavily involved with the Norman family.'

'What's this leading up to then, guv?' said Hansler, growing more nervous by the minute.

'You know that the Normans' only child, Alison, has been kidnapped?'

'Couldn't help knowing, could I, the way all the papers have been making a meal of it, appealing to the kidnappers' better nature and all that cobblers.'

'Didn't it ever occur to you that it was a strange coincidence, your wife killing herself within a day or two of Alison's abduction?'

'Well, pardon me for being thick, guv, but I just don't see the connection. What point are you trying to make?'

'Our line of thinking runs like this,' explained Scamp patiently. 'As soon as news was released that Alison Norman had been kidnapped, your wife ran away and hid in some flop-house under an assumed name. When we found her she was obviously terrified of something or somebody. She killed herself rather than submit to any more questioning. We think she must have known something, or suspected something about the crime. Probably she had a good idea who'd done it, and as he was close to her she was bound to become involved. Rather than endure the agony of that, she killed herself. As you were her husband, the only man we can find who's been that close to her, and as you've got a prison record with eight convictions for assorted felonies, we're bound to come asking you questions.'

Hansler had slowly turned grey with fear.

'That's not right, guv,' he protested. 'You've got no right to come after me for a thing like this, just because I've nicked a thing or two in my time and always paid my debt. I've never hurt anybody, couldn't do it. Non-violent, that's me. If

Helen ever thought I snatched the Norman girl, she must be barmy. Besides, Fred Cowie and his wife Angie can tell you I've never been away from my digs here. Not one night in the last twelve months. If I kidnapped that girl, where would I keep her? You tell me. In this house, for Christ's sake? You go and look under my bed.'

'I don't think you kidnapped her,' said Scamp. 'There's somebody else involved, and Helen had a good idea who it is. By that reckoning, I think you must know too because you were her husband for a few years. You must know as much about her as anybody.'

'That doesn't follow, guv. She was twenty-five when I married her, no pure white virgin. In fact I always knew she put it about. She was a hell of a sexy woman in those days. She'd had plenty of blokes before me. No sweat.'

'Give me a few names then,' said Scamp.

'How can I, guv? After all this time? You can't expect me to remember all that far back.'

'I'll tell you what I do expect,' said Scamp grimly. 'There's a sixteen-year-old girl held prisoner somewhere. Abused, probably maltreated and frightened out of her mind by some gruesome creep. I expect you to do everything in your power to help us find her quickly. If you refuse, I'll refresh your memory by taking you in on suspicion. We can hold you up to forty-eight hours without a charge, and then re-arrest you on the discovery of new evidence. The nick could be your home for quite some time.'

Hansler stared at him in terror.

'You wouldn't do that, guv. It's not right. I couldn't go back inside again. I had a nervous breakdown last time.'

'Tell me about the other men in Helen Webster's life. Tell me why she killed herself. What are you protecting? What have you got to lose? The woman's dead. You can't protect her any more. Did you know that while she was married to you and employed as Norman's secretary, she was having an affair with him?'

Hansler curled his lip, sour and resentful.

'Yeah, I knew all about it. That's why I got back at him in the only way I knew how, through his lousy money-bags. I robbed the bastard blind for years, all the time he was robbing me, and I didn't care what happened to me. Naturally when he found out what I was doing he called in the law and had me done for it. But he couldn't be sent to stir for the way he was robbing me. There's your even-handed justice! I've been on the skids ever since and ended up here. And when you come to weigh it up, it was all down to that bloody woman I married. She ruined my life.'

'What about her other men?' persisted Scamp patiently. 'You knew all about her and Norman, and you've implied he wasn't the only one.'

'Funny thing,' muttered Hansler, 'the way you fool yourself over a woman. I'd heard all the rumours about her, but I didn't believe them because I didn't want to. Funny thing what it does to your judgement when you just want to have it away with some bird. There was one story I heard about her that she'd lived with a bloke before me or Norman ever knew her. But he wasn't the marrying kind, certainly not to a tart who'd give it him for free. So when she told him she was up the spout, he just pissed off. When Helen started to swell, she cleared out to some old aunt up in the North, had the baby there, and got it adopted. Then she came back to town all bright and breezy and fancy-free, didn't she? In the marriage market, and butter wouldn't melt in her mouth. I was the poor sucker who fell for it, and took her on with all that behind her. No wonder I got screwed rotten by her and Norman.'

'How long is it, would you say, since she had this illegitimate baby?' said Scamp.

'Must be at least twenty years. More, because I've known her twenty years, and it was before then.'

'This is very important,' said Scamp. 'Can you give me the name of the man who lived with her and fathered this illegitimate child?'

'Yeah,' muttered Hansler resentfully. 'It was Prewitt, George Prewitt. The bastard!'

'Have you ever seen him or heard of him since?'

'No fear. I reckon you'd have to look for him in the Soho whore clubs and porn theatres. He'll have ponced his way into the big time by now.'

Scamp gave the poor old bum a couple of quid for his information, and the two detectives went back to London looking for a new milestone on the quest, Helen Webster's old lover, George Prewitt.

This time it was Scamp's connection in the Inland Revenue who quickly located Prewitt, for he was a successful advertising executive with a fine country house on the green slopes of the North Downs near Sevenoaks.

Prewitt had two lovely children at boarding schools, and a wealthy wife of French extraction called Yolande. He was a well preserved, handsome man in his fifties, a snazzy dresser and a plausible talker, as smooth as shot silk. If he was temporarily embarrassed by two detectives from the Met. suddenly homing in on him, he didn't show it. He welcomed them urbanely into his elegant book-lined study, which was better equipped for social drinking and entertaining than for scholarly pursuits.

Scamp curtly declined the offer of a drink and came straight to the point.

'Helen Webster. Does the name mean anything to you?'

Prewit stared at him blankly, searching the files of his memory for a fix on all the women he'd been through.

'If you read the *Evening Standard* you must have seen the report of her suicide a few days ago in a small paragraph on the inside. We have it on good authority that you lived with her once, before she was married, and fathered a baby on her.'

'Ssh!' hissed Prewitt nervously. 'Please lower your voice. My wife is in the house.'

'You mean you have secrets from her?' grinned D. C. Burgess. 'Like details of your horny past?'

'She owns the house,' replied Prewitt irritably. 'I like to live in peace.'

'Did you ever meet Helen Webster again after she'd had the baby?' pursued Scamp.

'Yes, we went out several times. She

was still hooked on me,' said the middle-aged Romeo, smoothing down his silvery thinning hair with complacent conceit.

'Then you must know what happened to the child.'

'Of course I know. She had him adopted into a very good home, gave him to her sister Ethel. Who else?'

'Her sister!' exclaimed Scamp. 'We were informed her sister emigrated to Australia many years ago.'

'That's right. She married an Aussie out there, but it didn't work out. So she got a divorce and came home. Then she remarried to a parson called Godaseth, some kind of a do-gooder in the New Cross Lewisham district. The Reverend Adrian Godaseth. Funny how you never forget a name like that. Poor Ethel was barren, yearning for babies, and suddenly there's her naughty, good-time sister Helen with this lovely baby boy casually churned out, a by-product of pleasure. Well, Helen couldn't afford to keep it and couldn't bear to lose it for ever by handing it over to some bureaucratic adoption society. So Ethel and her husband adopted the baby legally as their son, with the agreement that Helen could have access to see him whenever she wanted to. Absolutely the best kind of compromise all round.'

'Do you know where this vicar Godaseth lives now?'

'I can't say I do,' replied Prewitt smugly. 'He didn't exactly see eye to eye with a poor worldly sinner like me. You could say we were not quite *sympathique*. While the Godaseths lived in New Cross, I know Helen was always popping over to see her baby, and understandably the Godaseths got uptight about it. They didn't want an emotional tug of war with the natural mother over the child whom they'd come to regard as theirs. So they moved right away, across to the other side of London somewhere, and Helen found it much more difficult to get over there. I believe the Reverend Adrian took a living in Brentford, where there are plenty of deprived heathens to make him his ritualistic bed of nails.'

'What about the boy?'

'He must have grown up by now,' replied Prewitt indifferently.

'Haven't you ever seen him? Didn't you take an interest in him as his father, and watch him growing up, if only from a discreet distance?'

'Good God, no!' exclaimed Prewitt flippantly. 'A by-blow is a by-blow, old boy. Once known, best forgotten. No little bastard's going to thank his well-meaning sire for suddenly popping up in his well ordered life and saying: 'I'm your real Pappy. Love me for begetting you in a golden moment.' It just makes them vicious with the knowledge of all those years of rejection. Besides, I was satisfied the Godaseths were doing a grand job with his upbringing, so I gave them all my paternal blessings from afar. He carried my name, you know. Helen had him christened Arthur George Prewitt, though of course when he was officially adopted he took the surname Godaseth.'

'Well, thank you for your information,' said Scamp. 'I wouldn't let your wife know about your natural connection with the name Godaseth, if I were you. It

146

could start to stink before long.'

The two detectives drove away, leaving a distinctly uneasy George Prewitt to cook up a plausible explanation of their visit for his cynical and possessive French wife.

'What do you think then, skipper?' said Burgess. 'Do you fancy that creep's by-blow for Alison's kidnapping? He's a viable age, and as Helen Webster's son, he'd know all about the Norman finances and the Norman household. I reckon Helen knew enough about her own son to judge him capable of the crime, and that's why she did herself in as soon as we turned the heat on her. To my way of thinking, it's as open as a flasher's raincoat.'

'I'm beginning to think so too,' said Scamp grimly. 'Let's go and locate this Reverend Godaseth and his boy Arthur. Will you check the birth at Saint Catherine's House? Verify the registration of Arthur George Prewitt. Then look up the Church Register or the Anglican Communion, wherever C. of E. vicars are inventoried, and find out the whereabouts of the Reverend Adrian Godaseth, if he's still above ground. I'm going to check the files of all offenders brought up under the Children's and Young Persons' Act in the past ten years to find out if this Arthur Godaseth has some kind of juvenile crime record. There must be something down to him if he scared his mother into her grave.'

Back at Squad H.Q. they went to work, and D. C. Burgess soon had some answers. Arthur George Prewitt (father unknown) had been born to Miss Helen Prewitt in the Salford General Hospital twenty-two years ago. The birth had been duly recorded at the Registry of Births, Marriages and Deaths in Manchester.

The Reverend Adrian Godaseth, M.A.(Oxon), formerly curate at St. Faith's, New Cross, and later incumbent of St. Peter's Parish in Brentford, Middlesex, was now Vicar of All Souls in the Surrey stockbroker belt, an affluent congregation of middle-class virtues, far removed from the poor working-class parish where he'd first begun his cure of souls.

9

Scamp drove down alone through the park-like countryside, past Merton and Banstead to the pretty woodland village, reflecting grimly that it was within a twenty-mile radius of the lonely heath that the kidnapper had designated for handing over the ransom money.

Scamp took stock of the wealthy, expanding community, with its sixty-thousand-pound homes and its new red brick Victorian Gothic church that seemed to offer a conveniently aseptic road to salvation. The spruce neo-Georgian vicarage stood inside a walled garden nearby, and the Reverend Adrian Godaseth was in his study with his black stock and dog collar removed and his soft shirt open at the neck, enjoying an early afternoon whisky and soda before he got down to the wearisome chore of writing a sermon skilfully attuned to the sensibilities of the smug, self-satisfied, over-privileged pagans of this parish, who knew they were the Lord's Elect, saved without their effort.

Scamp realised it was going to be fairly tricky talking to a man of the cloth on the premise that his adopted son of twenty-two was a callous criminal who was inevitably going down for a long time.

The clergyman was tall and angular, with a shock of iron-grey and a pointed beard streaked with grey. He was a man of trendy ideas and Boy Scout enthusiasms and a vague, pompous manner. He tried to get through to the young people of his parish by having all the choir boys call him Adrian, by lifting an elbow in the public bar of the local pub, 'The Cricketers,' by sponsoring rowdy disco's at the Church Hall, and by blessing the Punk Rockers' motor bikes in church on Palm Sunday and Harvest Festival. He was a young and vigorous fifty-eight with a hearty and slightly patronising manner and a limp handshake.

'Bless my soul,' he exclaimed, gazing at Scamp's warrant card. 'A detective sergeant from the Metropolitan Police making forays into my humble parish! Whatever can be going on? I'm afraid we don't go in for big crimes here. No one has stolen the chalice or the communion wine, or broken into the Poor Box since I've been an incumbent here, my dear Watson, or should I say Holmes?'

Scamp found himself slightly irritated by the Reverend Godaseth's condescending facetiousness, and that made his task easier.

'Mr. Godaseth, I think you have a son by adoption, Arthur George Godaseth.'

'Certainly I have.'

'Do you know where he is at the moment?'

'I think I should do. He's away at college. The autumn term began there a couple of weeks ago.'

'Which college would that be?'

'Lisvane Theological College just outside Guildford. He's in his third year there, reading for the General Ordination Examination. He is following my footsteps into the Church, you see.'

'Less than thirty miles away over on the other side,' mused Scamp.

'I beg your pardon.'

'Is it a residential college?'

'Of course. But students are allowed a degree of freedom to go home at the week-ends if they so wish.'

'Does your son own a motor cycle?'

'No. He had one some years ago when he was sixteen, but he had an accident and broke his leg. His mother and I prevailed on him, for our peace of mind, to give up the motor cycle and rely on public transport.'

'Does he have a dog, like a Dobermann Pinscher for instance?'

'Of course not! What a ridiculous question. How would one keep a beast like that at a theological college? Might one ask the purpose behind these bizarre questions? What is your interest, as a police officer, in my son?'

'Is it true that he's not an anonymous waif from some Church of England Adoption Society, but the illegitimate son of your wife's sister, Helen Webster, recently deceased?'

The atmosphere grew distinctly frosty, and the Reverend Godaseth pursed his thin, hair-encrusted lips in heavy disapproval of Scamp.

'Your questions are now verging on the gratuitous and are becoming offensive, officer,' he said coldly. 'But yes. What you've just said is perfectly true. I would dearly like to know the source of your information, and your reason, if any, for seeking it.'

'I've been looking up the record of young offenders under the Children's and Young Persons' Act,' said Scamp. 'I notice that when your son was twelve years old he was in trouble for setting fire to his school over in Brentford, doing a hundred thousand pounds' worth of damage. He was remanded for psychiatric reports, and a slight psychopathic tendency was diagnosed. But they didn't consider it serious enough for him to be detained under the Mental Health Act. He was released into your care under the supervision of a probation officer. As far as the record shows, he's committed no other offences since. Have you noticed any further anti-social tendencies in Arthur during the past ten years?'

'Certainly not,' said Godaseth, bridling indignantly. 'There's also an understandable reason why he set fire to that school.'

'Really?' said Scamp. 'A justification for arson?'

'He hated the place. It was a huge rough shambles of a comprehensive school with a large immigrant population and a high incidence of theft, bullying and vandalism. What is known in educational circles, I believe as a Social Priority School. My wife and I sent him there mistakenly, thinking we were doing our democratic duty as modern, socially aware parents in trying to avoid the barriers of race and class. We never dreamed he was unhappy there until he made his own cry for help in his own way.'

Scamp raised his eyebrows at the trendy euphemism.

'Also it was at that time we judged it suitable to tell him that we were not his natural parents; that he was in fact our nephew by birth but our son by adoption. He was upset by the revelation, and became quiet and withdrawn. He started

154

showing a marked hostility towards my wife, and the whole family relationship was never as close and happy again. It's arguable of course that we ought not to have afflicted him with the knowledge. But right or wrong, he had to know in the end. The truth can't be suppressed. It was a part of his growing up.'

'Did he ever know his real mother?'

'Of course. She used to come and visit us often at New Cross when he was a small boy. Later on the visits stopped.'

'Was that at your insistence?'

'Yes, it was. I judged it would make him even more disturbed if this conflict of loyalties was forced on him between his natural mother and his social parents. She could never have given him the kind of home he enjoys here, and she was responsible enough to bow out for his sake.'

'I take it that he knows she's dead?'

'Of course.'

'Did he show any emotion?'

'None whatsoever. She might have been a stranger or a distant relative killed in a street accident.'

'Well, Mr. Godaseth, I have to tell you that his name has cropped up in certain enquiries of a serious nature. I have to see him at once.'

'What enquiries?' said Godaseth sharply. 'Are you going to his college?'

'Of course.'

'But is that really necessary? Think how it will look, an ordinand in his final year, looking to ordination, to be visited at college by a detective. Goodness knows what the college dignitaries and his bishop are going to think. He'll have a black mark against his name before he even starts his ministry. Couldn't you meet him here discreetly at the week-end to ask your questions?'

'I'm sorry,' said Scamp. 'Things are far too serious to hang about observing niceties. To put it bluntly, your son is a suspect in the kidnapping of Alison Norman which has aroused nationwide concern. You must know about it.'

'Incredible,' gasped the Reverend Godaseth. 'It's sheer fantasy. I don't believe it.'

'We've traced a direct family connection. Your sister-in-law, Helen Webster, was housekeeper to the Normans for twelve years. She didn't run away and kill herself at the news of the kidnapping for no reason. We think the man who telephoned about the ransom demand is educated and is in your son's age group. He used a biblical turn of phrase which made us wonder if he could be a theological student. That's why I have to question Arthur George Godaseth at once.'

'Please!' said the clergyman desperately. 'How can I persuade you? Please don't humiliate him at his college. You'll find your suspicions groundless anyway, and then an apology will be pointless after you've smeared him.'

'I'm sorry,' said Scamp formally.

He opened the study door brusquely on his way out, and almost fell into the arms of a woman who'd been listening at the key-hole. She was plump and well groomed and she dressed the part in tweed skirt, beige twin-set and a rope of pearls. She bore a certain facial resemblance to the ill-fated Helen Webster, but her looks were better preserved on account of her easier and more cosseted life.

She started fearfully and looked at Scamp with a dumb, pleading expression, as if trying to tell him something without speaking.

'Yes, what is it, my dear?' said the Reverend Godaseth testily.

'I — I'm sorry, Adrian,' she stammered. 'I wondered if you'd forgotten about the Harvest Festival Committee meeting.'

'That's not until 4.30, more than two hours away, and I have a sermon to write,' snapped Godaseth. 'The officer is just leaving, Ethel. Have the goodness to conduct him to the door.'

As she opened the outside door for him Ethel Godaseth whispered furtively: 'I've something I must say to you. Can you come back here after 4.30?'

Scamp nodded briefly and walked away down the garden path to the door in the wall. He was reluctant to hang about here for two hours when he had so much to do, but an unsolicited offer to talk to the police was such a rare bonus that he couldn't pass it up. He'd never find a better informed witness than the adoptive mother of the suspect.

He sat in his car near the village green, writing up a report on his note pad, until the church clock chimed 4.30. Five minutes later the Reverend Godaseth came dashing through the garden door with his cassock billowing behind him en route for his meeting in the Church Hall. Scamp went back into the vicarage, not without a certain wry feeling of guilt at this sly assignation with the woman behind her husband's back.

'I was listening at the door,' she said breathlessly. 'I heard nearly all that you said in there. It's what I feared. As soon as you came and I knew who you were, I had a terrible fear that my worst nightmare was being realised. You see, my husband is a good man, but he lives in some ideal world of his own and refuses to face unpleasant facts. He won't admit it, but Arthur is definitely evil. My sister — God rest her! — knew it too.'

'Presumably you have good grounds for

that statement,' said Scamp.

'I heard you mention the incident of Arthur setting fire to his school. But there's something else far more terrible which isn't on his record because no charge was ever made.'

'That's what I was afraid of,' said Scamp.

'He was nine years old at the time, and my husband was incumbent at Brentford. Arthur used to play in Gunnersbury Park with two little girls aged three and four. Their mother, a divorcee, used to leave them with him while she went across to the public house. She knew that Arthur was reliable and fond of them. But one day when she came to find them they'd disappeared, and so had Arthur. They were found drowned half a mile away in the Thames, and Arthur had gone off to a football match. When the police questioned him he said he'd left them playing in the park. He didn't know they were going to the river, and it wasn't his fault. What horrified us and the police as well was Arthur's complete lack of concern, no shred of feeling or remorse, as if the deaths of those two poor little mites didn't matter.

'The mother swore that he'd taken them to the river and pushed them in. She said they'd never have wandered off so far alone. But Arthur just looked everybody straight in the eye, even when the police were rough with him, and said they were playing in the park. He stuck calmly to his story that he'd wanted to go to a football match, and he didn't see why he had to take two girls with him. I don't think the police believed him, and I'm sure the mother didn't. But nobody could prove he had any criminal intent. We shall never know what really happened. There were no witnesses who'd seen the children near the river.

'After that I could never regard Arthur as a healthy, happy child. I never trusted him again. I knew he was evil.'

'What about him burning down his school?' said Scamp. 'Do you go along with your husband's white-washing of that escapade?'

'Certainly not. It was just another example of Arthur's sheer wickedness.

161

When we made the mistake of telling him about his real parenthood, it was as if he positively hated me for wanting to be a mother to him after his own mother's rejection. He never spoke of it until he was sixteen, and then he said to me quite casually one day: 'My mother was a whore. I suppose she wanted to get rid of me because I was in the way when she wanted to take men to bed. So why did you encourage her in it by taking me off her hands?'

'I was quite speechless for a moment, and then I tried to tell him that the Rector and I had adopted him because we loved him and we had no children of our own.

'He said: 'I don't know what you mean by love. Everybody just does what they want to.'

'I said his mother hadn't wanted to get rid of him, but she couldn't give him much of a home because of her wastrel of a husband who went to prison. So she'd sacrificed her own feelings for Arthur's good, wanting him to be brought up in a secure and decent home.

'He said: 'You must be mad if you can believe that. My mother is a cow, and one of these days I'll tell her so.' '

'Did he know that she was living in the Normans' house at Dulwich?'

'Yes, he must have done. He saw her letters to me. When she killed herself, I knew it was because of him, her son who hated her.'

'When you read about the Norman kidnapping, did you realise these were the Normans who'd employed your sister as their housekeeper?'

'Of course.'

'And you never suspected that Arthur might be involved in it?'

'It was too fantastic even to consider. I refused to face it. But Helen must have known, and she couldn't face it either, so she killed herself. When I heard you announce yourself to my husband, I knew the worst; that you must suspect our son as well, and now we shall have to face it. He'd been back at college four days at the start of the autumn term when the kidnapping took place. We have no means of knowing that he didn't break out of his college on the night in question. Students are not supposed to leave college without an Exeat, but after all a college is a civilised place, far from being a secure fortress or a prison.'

'I'm obliged to you for your frankness,' said Scamp. 'What you've told me will be treated in the strictest confidence if it turns out that your son is innocent. But I'm bound to say your information reinforces our line of thinking in this case.'

'I didn't know what to do for the best,' she said, wringing her hands. 'I feel guilty of disloyalty to my husband in talking to you behind his back like this. But I had no choice. If Arthur has done this terrible thing, it can't be hidden. That poor girl has to be found and set free before she suffers any more.'

'One other thing,' said Scamp. 'Can you give me the names of any of his associates, men or women, who could be his accomplices? I think there's more than one person involved in this crime.'

'I'm sorry. I can't help you there. He had no friends in the village. He always went up to London for his social and leisure activities. He didn't want us to know anything about it. It seemed furtive and unfriendly, and I was rather hurt by it.'

10

Scamp and D. C. Burgess motored up the tree-lined drive to Lisvane Theological College on the outskirts of Guildford, and parked in the visitors' car park.

The college was a fairly new building, endowed and maintained by the Church Commissioners, built of mellow brown stone, small and compact round a square quadrangle on the model of an Oxford college. It had a crenellated gate tower, a chapel and a library, and the college porter in the gate-house wore a black gown like a court usher. He directed them up a staircase to a first-floor office, where they found the Censor, the college's disciplinary officer.

He was a short, tubby, square-shouldered, hard-faced cleric in gold-rimmed spectacles, with a sanctimonious, thin-lipped mouth, dressed in black soutane and white dog collar. He stared incredulously and his thin lips tightened in prim outrage as the detectives identified themselves and stated their business.

'Are you sure you've come to the right place?' he intoned. 'One of our young men a police suspect! Can there be a mistake of identity?'

Scamp assured him there was no mistake, and asked him for his personal opinion on Arthur Godaseth.

'I know very little about him, except that he's one of our senior students, and is fairly close to ordination,' said the cleric. 'He should be better qualified than most to eschew the Devil and his works. As it's only the defaulters, backsliders and other weaker brethren who habitually come to my notice on disciplinary grounds, it's surely a point in his favour that I'm not well acquainted with him.'

'We'd like to talk to him,' said Scamp, 'and we'd appreciate it if you could put a private room at our disposal.'

'Oh, very well,' said the Censor, throwing down his pen and swinging round in his swivel chair to consult a timetable pinned up on the wall. 'You'd better use this office for your purpose.'

He lifted a telephone and spoke to a secretary.

'Miss Biddle, would you go across to the main lecture hall — Church History under Doctor Bartlett — convey my apologies, and ask him to send Mr. Godaseth to my office at once. It's a matter of some urgency.'

After a wait of five minutes there was a timid knock on the office door, and a black-clad figure glided silently in on soft black shoes. The detectives had their first meeting with Arthur George Godaseth.

He was the tall, dark and handsome kind with a pale, well shaped face bearing a slight resemblance to his natural father, George Prewitt. He had long black hair and long sideburns, and he had the darkly smouldering eyes of a seer or a fanatic that went well with his long black soutane, the standard uniform of chastity and piety.

Although the student had the meekly folded hands, the bent head and deferential stance of ingrained humility, Scamp was quick to recognise the suppressed nervous energy, the sheer intensity of a volatile if not violent temperament. Was he a two-faced wastrel of good education, hiding his profligacy under a parson's gown, or was he a real villain?

'Ah, Mr. Godaseth,' said the Censor, staring at the young man with harsh disapproval, 'these men are from the Metropolitan Police, and they wish to confer with you. I hope, for the sake of the college's good name, that you will soon disabuse them of their untoward suspicions.'

He stalked out of his office with his hands clasped behind his back, his chin in the air, and a prim swishing of skirts.

Scamp sat down behind the desk in the Censor's swivel chair, while D. C. Burgess stood menacingly to one side of him facing the student. Scamp didn't mince his words. He said sternly:

'Arthur George Godaseth, I want to know the whereabouts of Alison Norman at once.'

The student's head came up with a jolt as if a spasm of shock had gone through him, but his dark eyes became opaque and expressionless as if he'd switched over to a well trusted and well integrated defence mechanism.

'I'm sorry,' he said politely, not at all worried or scared. 'I don't know what you're talking about.'

'You deny all knowledge of the Norman family of Court Lane, Dulwich?'

'I don't know them,' said the student firmly.

'That's rather strange, considering your natural mother, Helen Webster, was housekeeper there for a good many years. Your adoptive mother was under no doubt that you knew all about the Norman connection.'

Godaseth smiled superciliously.

'Dear old Auntie Ethel,' he said. 'You'd get a good line in character assassination from her. She's always been against me.'

'So you lied then. You do know the Normans. You know of their wealth, and you know they have an only daughter.'

'You say so,' replied Godaseth coolly. 'It doesn't matter much what I say.'

'You don't seem to realise what serious trouble you're in,' observed Scamp. 'We're not talking about a traffic offence

170

or flashing on the common. When did you first get the idea of snatching Alison Norman for ransom?'

'I absolutely deny that I did,' said Godaseth, staring back at him with his opaque, expressionless gaze.

'Who else is in it with you? Who owns the Dobermann?'

'Dobermann?' said Godaseth blankly.

'We found the hairs of a Dobermann Pinscher on Alison's overcoat that you or your accomplice restored to the parents.'

'I don't understand.'

'Do you ride a motor cycle?'

'I don't possess a motor cycle. How would a poor student existing on a C.A.C.T.M. grant, with no extra money from a skinflint father be able to run a motor cycle?'

'That wasn't what I asked. Can you ride a motor cycle?'

'I suppose so. Can't everybody these days?'

'I think you must know that the game's up, Godaseth,' said Scamp grimly. 'You can't possibly collect that ransom now. You saw what happened when you tried

171

to pick it up the other night. Your only possible course now is to return the girl and trust that she gives you a good recommendation for gentlemanly treatment. If she's unharmed, it could make all the difference between a seven-year sentence and a fifteen-year stretch.'

'You're completely mistaken throwing all these wild charges about,' said Godaseth still unruffled.

'What made you do it? Was it because the Normans had treated your natural mother badly, or just greed for ready money? You knew the Normans were loaded, and how fond they are of Alison.'

'I don't know Alison Norman, I tell you. I'm studying for the Ministry of the Church. Why should I jeopardise everything for such a wild, desperate scheme as to stage a kidnapping?'

'You tell me,' said Scamp. 'If I knew all the crazy contortions of the criminal mind I wouldn't be a copper. I'd be God. Where were you on the night of September 20th?'

'I was here, of course, sitting up late in

my study, reading my Church Doctrine and Pastoralia.'

'Can anybody vouch for that?'

'The college porter, I suppose. Everyone has to sign the book at the lodge whenever they leave college, and sign in again when they return. The gates are locked at ten o'clock. It's a disciplinary charge incurring a fine or suspension to be out after hours. You'll find no record that I've ever been disciplined.'

'You could have climbed out through a window,' said Scamp. 'This place doesn't strike me as being up to maximum security standards. Show us where you sleep.'

Obediently Godaseth led them downstairs and across a quadrangle which was now populous with other students on their way to and from lectures in their long black skirts. They gave veiled, curious glances at Godaseth, who was considered a loner and a creep, and was generally to be seen standing decorously with eyes downcast and hands meekly folded imbibing the paternal wisdom of some bent old cleric in black cloak and square biretta. Godaseth scorned the silly mob loyalty and vulgar camaraderie of his fellow students. So now when they saw him walking between two large strangers with big policemen's feet and grim faces, who had an air of irresistible authority, they perked up with the pious hope that perhaps the college creep was in real trouble at last.

The study was on the first floor of the west wing. It was little more than a cell, with naked brown stone walls whose only ornament was a wooden crucifix and a long mirror on one wall. Scamp thought this a rather incongruous appurtenance for the bleak austerity of an anchorite's cell. There was a functional iron bedstead, a varnished deal chair and table, and a couple of shelves for theological books. The window was a small Gothic shaped casement which opened outward on the college grounds and gardens. There were three vertical iron bars on the inside to prevent enterprising and wordly souls from climbing out into the gay world to enjoy the fleshpots when they should have been praying.

Scamp looked closely at the screws which secured the bars to the woodwork. The heads looked scratched and shiny as if somebody had recently worked on them. In a drawer of the table he found a small general purpose screwdriver which told him all he needed to know.

Outside there was a drop of about twenty feet to a well-kept lawn, and conveniently close to the window for any agile climber there was a stout, square, cast iron drainpipe securely bolted to the stone wall.

'You've been out through this window more than once,' said Scamp. 'I bet we'd find your palm prints all over that drainpipe if we had it dusted.'

'Is it a police matter to climb out of college?' said Godaseth plaintively.

'Anybody who could climb in and out of this window would have no difficulty in climbing into the Normans' house. Where do you keep your black crash helmet, black jacket and boots?'

'Probably where he's got Alison stashed,' said Burgess. 'What's more to the point, where does he keep his motor bike?'

'We're taking you in for further

175

questioning, Godaseth,' said Scamp. 'We shall want all your clothes for forensic examination, just to make sure you've not collected any of the Dobermann hairs that were on Alison's overcoat.'

Watching the student's face closely, Scamp was sure he saw a flicker of relief and smug, triumphant satisfaction in the intense dark eyes.

'It's a complete waste of time taking me to any police station,' said Godaseth vehemently. 'And think what it'll do to my career. Even though I'm innocent, mud always sticks. The College Board have discretionary powers to ask anyone they think unsuitable to withdraw his name from the books. If I'm arrested here by the police, even on such absurd grounds as you've got, they're bound to question whether I'm suitable material for the Ministry.'

'They'd be right to question it too, wouldn't they?' retorted Scamp. 'Do you really need a career in the Church when there are so much more kicks and profit in a life of crime? Tell us where Alison is, and it'll be a lot easier for you. We might even be able to drop most of it on your accomplice.'

'I don't know Alison, I tell you,' said Godaseth with a desperate whine of injured innocence. 'I have no idea where she is.'

'Start packing,' said Scamp, 'everything down to your last dirty shirt and your lace-trimmed cotta. Geoff, go and inform the College Brass that we're taking off with one of their *novitiates*.'

'It won't be long before these old prelates tip off his father that he's been lifted,' said Burgess. 'Then we'll have a smart lawyer in our hair, impeding the course of justice.'

11

'There's no joy from Forensic,' said Earwacker morosely, studying the laboratory report on Godaseth's clothes. 'Micro-particles of lead and carbon in his trousers. He could have got that from standing too near a car's exhaust in the street. Funny thing though, his black parson's soutane is practically brand new. Not a trace of anything on it, except a whiff of church incense. I wonder what happened to his old cassock. I mean it's not the kind of garment you buy very often. They must cost about fifty quid a time, so I reckon the average theological student would buy just one and make it last him a lifetime. Why did Godaseth need a new one in his third year?'

'Maybe he keeps a spare one for his criminal activities,' suggested Scamp. 'A lot of clergy are fetishists about wearing their cassocks everywhere they go. The bent ones probably feel respectable about committing crimes if they're absolved in advance by the garb of sanctity. I can't somehow see Godaseth climbing down that drainpipe in a cassock, so if he needs one to sanctify his criminal life, he'll have a spare one that he keeps presumably at his base of operations, where he's got Alison stashed away. No wonder he looked relieved and smug when I said we were going to examine his clothing. He knew he was fire-proof.'

'Isn't that a sod!' exclaimed Earwacker bitterly. 'Not a damned thing on him. We've got absolutely nothing to take to the Prosecutor's Office, so we shall have to let him go after forty-eight hours. That smart solicitor hired by his father is raising hell as far up the ladder as he can get. Being a college boy in training for the Ministry is an almost perfect alibi. And Godaseth's clammed up as tight as the hardest villain. He just sits there with folded hands and downcast eyes, and that injured, self-righteous look, as if he knows we'll never get anywhere. Either we've got the wrong man, or he's buried Alison where he knows she'll never be found. Sometimes I have an awful feeling that she's already dead and will never surface. So without Godaseth's confession, we'll never break this case.'

'It's got to be him,' said Scamp. 'I was never surer of anything in my life. If only we could conjure a few of those Dobermann hairs from Alison's overcoat on to Godaseth's trousers, we'd have him bang to rights.'

'Lay off,' growled Earwacker. 'They'd have your balls even for the thought. We're in the era of the Thought Police now. Remember how a big career was destroyed because of the one word 'wog', spoken at a private dinner party and recorded by some creep with a cassette? Well, don't incriminate me with talk about planting evidence. What about the enquiries at garages in the Guildford area about Godaseth hiring a motor bike?'

'Negative so far,' replied Scamp. 'As you'd expect, he'd be fly enough to hire his bike in the Smoke, and you know how long it's going to take to check that lot.'

'Is it worth keeping him here for the permitted forty-eight hours?' said Earwacker. 'Or shall we turn him loose and cut our losses?'

'What's your own personal impression of him?' said Scamp. 'Is he just an odd ball, or is he driven by some madness that defies medical definition? Funny thing that he should want to be a parson.'

'Is it? I'd call it damned good tactics. What better front could you have for a life of crime than that of a milk-and-water, canting parson, with all the leisure time to do your rip-offs in between baptising babies and praying over stiffs? Not even the police would suspect it could be the one virtuous man in the community. Remember the case of that West Country vicar who teamed up with his house-keeper to rip off the big country houses round about? And when the Regional Crime Squad did get a line on him, they couldn't believe it. Not till they found the Aladdin's Cave of stolen valuables in his vicarage.'

'We can release Godaseth and keep him under surveillance,' said Scamp. 'Sooner or later he's going to lead us to the secret retreat where Alison is, and to his accomplices.'

'Why should he, if Alison is dead?'

'They could still make another bid to get the ransom money from Norman,' rejoined Scamp. 'Nobody can be sure she's dead until her body is found. Besides, they'll have a taste for it now. We can be safe in assuming that they're all greedy sods with the dream of big money, so why should they be permanently discouraged by one bungled attempt? They wouldn't have to look far for somebody else who's loaded, with a daughter or a wife he dotes on and ready to pay up all he's got to bring her home safely.'

'But it could be weeks or months before they sus somebody else out,' objected Earwacker. 'I'll put a man on watching the college, but Godaseth won't lead us anywhere now he knows we're on to him. He can be in touch with his accomplices by letter or telephone. I don't think it very likely that they'll let us bug the phone at that college.'

'Nor do I. But we know the kidnappers' operational area is in a twenty-mile radius, taking in Leatherhead, Dorking,

Reigate and Guildford. If we could find out from the Kennel Club every registered owner of a big dog in that area, every registered guard dog and ex-police dog that's been retired into private ownership, every vet who's ever treated a Dobermann; if we could trace all the dog breeders and kennels proprietors, and check them all out for some employee or relative with a criminal record, we might, with a bit of luck, come across the man whose Dobermann rubbed up against Alison's overcoat.'

'Tracing a single bloody dog in a nation of dog-loving idiots,' grumbled Earwacker. 'It's not much of a chance. Villains aren't likely to be law-abiding when it comes to buying a dog licence.'

'Apart from waiting for Godaseth to lead us home, it's the only line we have,' replied Scamp.

'Well, I'll put it to the guv'nor. The Regional Crime Squad in Surrey will have to be brought in on it.'

12

Arthur Godaseth was released after the maximum time of forty-eight hours that he could be held without a charge. He went away, escorted by his solicitor, still clad in his black soutane, still with eyes humbly cast down and the resigned forbearing look of martyred innocence, as if he readily forgave all those who had despitefully used him, because they knew not what they did.

Through long hours of harsh interrogation, he had admitted nothing, seeing through all the verbal traps and trick questions they'd set for him, sensing their frustration and anger at his impassiveness. They couldn't intimidate or goad him or provoke him because he knew their game and he was cool. Not weakening or giving anything away under bullying pressure was the true professionalism.

He knew the detectives were so

desperate to find Alison that they would gladly have beaten the truth or the life out of him, if they hadn't feared the vigilance of Mr. Piers Thraplestone, the sharp lawyer who'd been hired to protect him.

So he went back through the saintly portals into the calm unworldly atmosphere of devoted priests and pseudo-priests and time servers who knew a cushy number when they saw it. He had a brief interview with the Censor and the Warden and was able to convince them with his usual glib plausibility and air of natural piety that it had all been a terrible mistake. The police had been over-reacting in their hamfisted zeal to find a missing girl. They thought they'd traced a tenuous lead to him because his mother's sister had once worked as a housekeeper for the missing girl's parents many years ago. They'd eliminated him from their enquiries when they found no evidence against him.

The Warden commiserated with Godaseth and declared the incident closed. Godaseth went immediately to the college bath-house and sluiced himself down to clear away the prison filth. His lonely spartan cell in the college was like a pure, clean bower compared with the sleazy, noisome repressiveness of the prison cell where they'd locked him up for two days. There was a song in his heart that he'd beaten the cack-handed fuzz.

Back from his hot bath he stripped off his dressing gown and stood naked in front of the long mirror, preening himself, drooling with self-love, for he was an obscene fetishist. He had a well thewed, muscular body with a virile growth of black hair on his chest. Further down was nature's supreme endowment, the symbol and guarantee of his masculinity, bull-like and seething with power. From pre-adolescent years he'd tended it, anointed it with perfume and watched it grow, like a fond gardener with a favourite orchid. If the Warden and all the other sternly repressed clerics on the College Board could have had any idea of the antics he got up to in the serene privacy of his monk's cell, they would have stormed there in force with bell, book and candle to exorcise their evil acolyte.

It was in London during the vacations that Arthur Godaseth really indulged his dark satanic powers. He had a special delight in young, nubile girls, irrespective of race, colour or looks, whom he found in the coffee-bars and disco's, and hanging about the pubs in the newly created slums of inner city decay and deteriorating tower blocks. Adolescent greenness and innocence were everything. If they submitted to his gross indecencies without a struggle, so much the better. But if they fought him, he belted them into abject surrender, and his victorious violence turned him on to even wilder euphoria and excess. Under cover of darkness, in the semi-desert of housing rubble and newly made municipal gardens, there was generally so much vandalism and mayhem going on after dark that nobody came to investigate Godaseth's own modest enterprise in the shadows.

His first woman had been a thirty-year-old virgin, when he was fourteen. She was a newly-appointed assistant matron at the expensive boarding school for the sons of clergy on the Sussex coast. One night he slipped out of the dormitory and crept along the dimly lighted corridor to her room. She was asleep as he put his hand over her mouth and slipped into her bed.

When he'd finished and she was sobbing with shame and fear, he said: 'If you tell anybody, the police will get you for seducing a schoolboy you're supposed to be looking after. There'll be a hell of a row, but you'll get the worst of it because you're old enough to know better.'

The woman saw his point and kept quiet, so Godaseth got away with it. He was now crazed with the arrogance of his sexual prowess, and took steps to continue gratifying his lust with discreet cunning. He had neither compassion nor remorse for his victims. Love of power complemented his sex drive, power over the weak and chicken-hearted who could be terrorised into compliance without complaint. Even though the other men of his cloth were like hungry paupers looking in on a feast, Godaseth wasn't going to be deprived of anything.

When his adoptive parents told him

who his mother was, and he worked it out that he was a bastard, he started to hate everybody for their pretensions to respectability. Above all he hated his natural mother with implacable self-righteousness for her inept and easy virtue. Not even to give him a natural father whom he could put the spurs to!

When he heard that she'd killed herself in a cheap hotel, he thought it was bloody good riddance. He didn't want a loose end like a whore for a mother cluttering up his life.

★　★　★

It was Davinia Brutnell who really shaped his destiny, and put him on the road to power. It happened during the Easter vacation in his second year at Lisvane Theological College. One night he'd wandered all over Battersea Park looking for an easy victim, and he went into a pub near the Embankment to recharge his batteries. It was a rather stuffy, sober-looking Victorian pub, with a stuffy and sober clientele, and Godaseth found

189

himself in a snug, heavily carpeted little bar with a white-coated barman at the counter.

There was a sparse sprinkling of quietly-dressed middle-aged citizens lying back in the easy chairs, sipping short drinks and talking in muted tones. There were some stools round the semi-circular bar counter, with two or three habitues talking sport, hunched in characteristic poses over their drinks and cigarettes. At the far end of the bar was an unattached woman with long blonde hair, a fashionable and expensive coat draped loosely over her shoulders, and her long fleshy legs carelessly crossed on the bar stool. Even a theological student could tell from her crocodile handbag and shoes and her general style that she lived and breathed in the ambience of wealth. She was smoking continuously and occasionally taking a pull at her vodka and lime. She could have been thirty or thirty-five, but she was very easy on the eye, and there was no mistaking the sultry pall of overhanging sexuality.

As Godaseth went to the counter

alongside her, she shot him a sidelong glance of interest in her hard, bright, emerald eyes. He felt the unmistakable prickle of a challenge, the lure of a kindred spirit and the magnetism of unrestrained evil.

Accommodatingly she uncrossed and recrossed her legs for Godaseth's benefit, and showed him she was wearing flimsy white gossamer knickers edged with lace a couple of inches above her stocking tops. For a long moment her eyes held his, questioning, daring, provocative and slightly mocking. As the new head of steam boiled up in him, he sat on the stool close beside her, elbow to elbow.

'Another drink?' he said.

'Thank you. Why not?' she replied coolly in her top drawer accent.

So Godaseth snapped his fingers at the lurking barman to bring another large vodka and lime.

'I had a little bet with myself as to whether you'd make a bid,' she said casually, 'and I won hands down. I'm never wrong about men. What line are you in?'

'I'm a student.'

Davinia slapped her knee and laughed heartily, displaying perfect teeth that were slightly dingy from tobacco smoke.

'I knew it,' she declared. 'Escaped. Out on the town and trying your fledgeling wings. Be careful, Sonny Jim. I might tell your mother.'

'Don't let appearances fool you,' said Godaseth. 'I've got about six years' good and varied experience behind me, and a big backlog of satisfied customers. You should ask the one I left ten minutes ago.'

'A big talker, eh?' scoffed Davinia. 'They're never worth a damn in my experience.'

He whispered a few obscene specifications in her ear, and she looked at him with renewed interest, a far-off sentimental glow in her green eyes.

'I don't believe you.'

'Take me to your place, and I'll prove it.'

'I might just do that, you cheeky young sod,' she laughed.

From that moment Godaseth knew

she'd accepted him as her new devotee, her acolyte and accomplice. She slowly exhaled tobacco smoke into his face and squeezed his thigh.

'Go and find a taxi,' she said in her blasé, imperious drawl. 'Let's see if you're worth your corn.'

So she took him home to her luxury flat in Bessborough Street, Westminster, with magnificent views over Vauxhall Bridge and the Albert Embankment.

In a bedroom upholstered with genuine Gobelin tapestry and a huge canopied bed with black silk sheets, she put him through his paces with the exacting demands of a real high roller.

'You'll do,' gasped Davinia at length. 'You're no empty boaster. What a waste to take that into the Church and hide it under a black gown.'

'It won't stay hidden for long,' he boasted. 'There are always plenty of deprived lady parishioners hanging round a young priest, not to mention the choir ladies and vestal virgins of the Sunday School.'

'Just as a matter of interest,' said

Davinia, 'why are you so dead set on being a vicar? I don't know much about the Cloth, but I would have thought you needed to be a man of high principle and small earthly appetites in order even to be half-way happy as a priest. They work for a skinflint corporation that's richer than the Mafia, and pays them hardly enough to exist on the poverty line. So what's a bloody hell-raising, worldly minded, womanising rogue like you — the least spiritual man I've ever met, if you can understand the term — doing among the Holy Men?'

'One has to have a profession,' he said with a shrug. 'It's a cachet of honour and respectability in this class-crazy country. I didn't do well enough at school to go in for a real profession like the law or medicine. I was too busy chasing girls and widening my sexual experience when I should have been swotting hard for my 'A' Levels.'

'I can believe that!'

'But as my old man was a pillar of the Church, and the Church had paid for my education, it was cut and dried that I'd be accepted by the Church Advisory Council for training for the Ministry. My father pushed it at me for all he was worth to take up the cross he'd always carried. As soon as I was old enough to add things up, I could see the advantages. So I've got my respectable front, and there'll be no shortage of fringe benefits, you can bank on it. Wealthy widows, lonely hearts, emotional unfulfilment, the need for a cool, sanctifying hand on a fevered matronly brow. It's a wonderful vocation for someone with my flair, who believes with Nietzsche that force is the first law, and struggle is the father of all things.'

'Yes,' said Davinia sourly. 'Society's going to deserve you, a bloody sex-mad vicar, Savonarola built like a stud horse! I can see you're going to have a whale of a time, till you overplay your hand and get unfrocked. A bloody fringe benefit, am I?'

'Oh, don't be like that, Davinia,' he said conciliatingly. 'From the first glimpse I had of you I knew you were something special. Am I allowed here again?'

'Well, I suppose so. I was always a

push-over for a good stud. And the older I get the more I realise that they're not easy to come by. With your credentials you've got a standing invitation, if you don't mind the risk of tangling with my drunken sot of a husband.'

'Husband!' exclaimed Godaseth in sudden alarm, for he'd taken it for granted that she was a self-sufficient divorcee or widow, not the sort who plied for hire, and a high-class tart only when somebody took her fancy. He didn't want the dangerous complication of a husband who might offer physical violence as well as scandal.

She looked into his eyes with a cynical smile, reading him like an open book and confirming her belief that she would be the dominant partner.

'Of course I've got a husband,' she said impatiently. 'Who do you suppose pays for all this? You wouldn't like to do him in for me, would you?'

At first he thought she was joking, and then he realised that he'd met somebody as ruthlessly amoral as himself.

'Why?' said Godaseth ironically. 'Have

you got him heavily insured?'

She explained that Derek Brutnell was a City banker, whose business was on the skids because he drank, gambled and whored too freely.

'At his present rate of expenditure,' she declared, 'by the time his cirrhosed liver does him in, there'll be hardly enough money left to bury him.'

'Tough luck,' replied Godaseth flippantly. 'I'm sorry I can't help you out. But I make it a rule not to help women dispose of their derelict husbands. By going to the police, they'd find it so easy to dispose of me afterwards.'

She laughed on a note of bitterness.

'That's good thinking, Arthur. I don't need convincing you have a pretty good eye to the main chance — a typical bloody vicar! So you'd better get your trousers on and make tracks. Derek is likely to be back any time now, and he's a vicious swine when he's drunk. You might have to dispose of him to save your own skin.'

★   ★   ★

Thus from his casual pick-up of Davinia Brutnell in a pub there developed through their sexual partnership a strengthening alliance of mutual need that could only lead to crime. They saw the world through the same pitiless eyes, with the same cynical hedonism and cruel selfishness. No computer dating or marriage agency could have found Godaseth a more suitable partner in the physical, amoral and brutal sense. Godaseth didn't believe in God, but he was forced to acknowledge that some interested Destiny had guided his steps to that pub on the embankment where Davinia Brutnell awaited him.

Godaseth met her in London two or three times a week during the vacation, and it was his need for her that first drove him to break out of the theological college at night by unscrewing the bars from his cell window and climbing down a drainpipe. He made his way to London on a hired motor bike, met Davinia at her flat, or at a small hotel if her husband was at home, and spent a few wild, orgiastic hours with her before roaring back to

Guildford in the early hours, leaving his motor bike in a hired lock-up, and climbing back into college in time for early Mass.

When this had been going on for over a year, Destiny took another hand in the game. Davinia's husband was found dead on a mattress in a squatters' house in Putney. He'd been summoned before the Bankruptcy Court, and his private banking activities were about to be investigated by the Fraud Squad. A skinful of alcohol and a massive dose of barbiturates seemed the best way out. The other squatters in the house were so used to seeing drunken bums flaked out among the decaying detritus that they took no notice of him till he started to look and smell horribly dead.

As she talked it over with her lover, Davinia regarded the disaster with cold anger rather than sorrow.

'What a bloody mess!' she exclaimed bitterly. 'I reckon he wished all this on me just for spite. The bastard! I've got to get out of the flat and not take so much as a bloody ash-tray with me. The Official

Receiver's got his thieving hooks into it, and everything's to be sold to give something back to the creditors.'

'Where will you go?' said Godaseth curiously.

'Back home to the ancestral ruin, I suppose. A senile father of eighty-six who crawls about in two rooms of a decaying manor house, with a couple of family servants as ga-ga as he is.'

'Whereabouts is it?'

'Out in the wilderness, beyond Leatherhead. I was born and grew up there. Provincial gentry, you know. They've all gone now, dead or cleared off abroad. The old man should have sold up years ago and gone into an Old Folks' Home while he still had some money.'

'Well, it can't be all bad if it's a manor house and you're the only inheritor,' said Godaseth thoughtfully. 'The old man's bound to pop off in a year or two, and then it'll be yours. You can sell it and live on the proceeds.'

'If only it was that simple!' exclaimed Davinia bitterly.

'What with death duties and the cost of

upkeep, the old man was right out of money ten years ago. There was already a hefty mortgage on the property, held by the bank. So a few years ago he signed the whole estate over to the bank in return for a life annuity. It enables him to go on existing there in old-world make-believe until his death, and then of course the house and everything in it will belong to the bank. Nothing in it for me except his debts. I shall be out on my neck from there within a year or two, say five years at the most, unless I can mummify him and pretend he's still alive.'

'You need to raise a lot of money fast,' suggested Godaseth.

'Don't I bloody well know it!'

They looked at each other, and Godaseth realised that there were no lengths to which she wouldn't go in order to maintain her rich and self-indulgent way of life. Not for the first time they had a long, earnest discussion on all the known ways of raising big money, with and without the risk of ending up in gaol. But it was no longer mere academic speculation for Davinia Brutnell. She really meant it this time. Inevitably she cast her envious eyes on the new rich, the entrepreneurial society, that eternal butt of life's failures, the bourgeoisie to which she belonged herself by birth, marriage and inclination.

'There are so many of the filthy rich,' declared Davinia resentfully, 'and they cling so tight to their money, with banks, police forces and armies to guard it for them. But basically they're all cowards. It only needs the slightest pressure on the right nerve to turn them into quivering jellies. Then they'll relax the purse-strings all right. That of course is the technique of the blackmailer. You don't have to attack Fort Knox if you can make the custodians willing to open it up.'

'It's just a question of finding the right nerve to stimulate,' mused Godaseth. 'You have to become privy to some dark, disgusting secret that the rich man will pay handsomely to keep concealed. And that means research, patience, investing time and ingenuity, paying people to find things out and risking that one's own agents may become blackmailers in their turn. Unless — '

'Unless what?' said Davinia sharply.

'My pastoral studies lead me to believe that perhaps one can work on the rich more easily through their simple affections rather than through their locked-up secrets. Every rich man has a family of sorts, a wife, a child, a parent to whom he's devoted, for whose safety it would be well worth while relaxing the purse-strings.'

'You mean taking a hostage for ransom?'

'Why not? It's become very fashionable in Italy, simply because it's so easy to bring off successfully. The police are hobbled and hamstrung by the sheer cowardice of the victim's wealthy relatives. They'll do anything, pay any amount rather than risk the death of the loved one.'

'My God,' said Davinia, looking at him admiringly. 'I wasn't wrong about you. You're a real sharp devil. That black skirt and dog collar will become you very well when you're finally loosed up among your wealthy parishioners, a fox in the chicken run. Did you have any particular client in mind?'

'Yes,' said Godaseth briskly. 'I know one who's tailor-made for paying a hefty ransom. He's rich. He runs a plastics factory in New Cross. One of your ruthless captains of industry who'd tyrannise his workers and use child labour if the tide of history hadn't gone past him. He deserves all that's coming to him. My mother was his housekeeper, until he fired her on some pretext. I've never met him, and he doesn't even know of my existence, but I've always hated him, ever since I found out who my natural mother was, working in his house, a menial and a whore. I could be his bastard for all I know, and for all he cares. Even if he knew I was, he wouldn't do a damned thing to help me. He's got one child, a miserable spoilt brat called Alison, the apple of his eye. He'd pay any amount of money to have her brought back safely. I know the house in Dulwich. It would be as easy as a walk in the park to go in there one night and come out with Alison. And if you're going to live in some decaying old manor house in the wilderness with one senile old man who doesn't know what time of day it is, we've got the ideal place to imprison her indefinitely. We could take our time arranging a safe handover of the ransom.'

He could almost see the wheels turning over behind Davinia's calculating eyes as she hung on his every word. The plan began to take form and substance as they worked over it together. They egged each other on. Each of them alone would probably have chickened out when confronted by the stark enormity of the crime they planned. But together they bolstered each other up with fire and resolution, each being afraid of the other's ridicule and contempt.

13

In Alison's lonely prison several days had passed since the rape by the hooded man. Nothing else had happened, and thankfully she did not see the rapist in his priestly garb again. She deduced that they didn't intend to kill her, or she would be dead by now. Therefore they must be keeping her alive with the intention of still collecting the ransom.

Alison still had periodic fits of sobbing whenever she remembered her gruesome ordeal. But she was psychologically on the mend because of her vengeful hatred and her obsessive determination to escape, so that she could turn the tables on her captors.

She had a plan and she was constantly rehearsing it in her mind, looking for the things that could go wrong. She'd been working hard to remove one of the stout mahogany legs from the old cane chair, which had been solidly built and did not yield easily. At first it only moved a tiny fraction in its well-mitred joint, but she kept on working away at it for hours until it gradually became looser and the movement was more pronounced. Eventually she was working it to and fro through ninety degrees, until at last the heavy chair leg was free in her hand.

She hid it under her mattress, and propped the three-legged chair up against the wall, convinced that Harold wouldn't notice one leg was missing because he couldn't count up to four.

Meanwhile she was using on Harold her female wiles, of which she was growing increasingly aware, to stimulate what long damped-down sexual fires burnt in her repulsive captor. She'd trained him to bring her a bowl of hot water each morning, and his reward was a fleeting glimpse of her young pointed breasts as she washed the top half of her body in his presence.

As he watched her, his eyes were no longer dull and expressionless. He'd found a purpose in life. There was a slowly brightening gleam of excited interest, as if his sight had been opened on a brave new world.

Observing him with calculating eyes, Alison was convinced that he'd never had a woman in all his deprived, twilight existence. But the primeval urge was there all right. She was gambling with disaster in tampering with it, but she felt now she had nothing left to lose. If Harold went mad and strangled her in a lustful brainstorm, so much the better.

Harold would watch her hungrily as she tantalised him with her ablutions, drooling and licking his lips, but it never occurred to him to come and take what he needed. He seemed to regard her as something untouchable.

Alison smiled at him, praised him, and kept reassuring him how much she liked him. She steeled herself to put her soft hand on his sallow, stubbly cheek and kiss his thin, ferrety lips. His breath stank like seaweed grown in a drain. It nearly made her sick on the spot, but she steeled herself to go through with it. She was going to get what she wanted by being a whore, because that was to be her rôle in life ever after, dangling as a baited snare what the male animal would snatch by force if he thought he could get away with it. She might as well practise her technique on Harold.

His eyes glowed crazily and he clutched at her with real hunger.

'Arrgh, you'm a little beauty!' he panted. 'Come 'ere!'

But Alison slipped nimbly away and admonished him severely.

'Now, Harold, that's not nice. You must be a gentleman, or I shan't be your friend. Don't snatch. Wait till it's given. Perhaps one day, if you go on being a good boy, I'll be really nice to you.'

'Arrgh, I'd like that, you bet,' panted Harold with the fervour of his new awakening.

She coaxed him along with instinctive subtlety, not offering too much or killing his interest with too little, always holding out the promise that one day soon she'd lie on the mattress with him and be really nice.

Every time Harold came in with a meal, he thought it was jackpot time and set the tray down, panting with excitement, until she gently disillusioned him.

She'd worked it out that her bid for freedom had to be made when it was dark. If she discounted the dog, she would be better able to elude pursuit in the darkness until she found help.

One night when Harold brought in her evening meal, she put her hands on his shoulders, looked into his small black eyes and said:

'Tonight's the night, Harold, you lucky boy. I'm going to be really nice to you tonight as a little reward for all you've done for me.'

'Arrgh, you little beauty!' he gloated. 'Let's be at it then.'

'All right, but don't be a greedy boy, Harold. I have to eat my tea first to get my strength up for you. Why don't you chain Rufus up while you're waiting? I can't be really nice to you while you're clutching that beast. He frightens me. Besides, he might bite me when I try to do something to you.'

Harold stared at her in obvious bewilderment.

'You could just loop the chain round that beam to keep him away from us,' she suggested, pointing to one of the massive oak uprights that supported the roof. 'Rufus might want to join in when he sees what fun we're having. We couldn't allow that, could we, Harold? Not while I'm being extra specially nice to you.'

Harold got the message at last, and eagerly wrapped the stout steel dog chain round the beam, putting the steel bar at the chain's end through a ring so that no amount of shaking could work it loose.

Alison noted with a feeling of mounting triumph that the radius of the chain would keep the hound well clear of her mattress and of the unlocked door.

'Come along then, Harold,' she murmured with a much rehearsed sultry look, patting the mattress beside her. 'Come and have your reward for being such a good boy.'

Resolutely she put her arms round his neck and kissed him passionately. It was like putting your hand in the fire or picking up a rat. You could force yourself when there was no other way.

Harold started to breathe in long gasps, trembling with uncontrollable excitement. Boldly she unbuttoned the front of his trousers and tentatively started doing what she'd heard the more shameless hussies at school boasting that they did when they were alone with boys in cinema seats or darkened disco's.

'Oooo, arrgh! I likes that,' chuckled Harold. 'Ooo, arrgh! That be champion!'

He clutched at her greedily, his grimy, calloused hands squeezing without finesse at her immature nipples, trying frenziedly to mount her as he forced her back on the mattress. His trousers and grimy underpants were down about his knees. He stank of old rancid sweat and even older tobacco. Whether he'd done it before or not, he certainly knew where he was going. Suddenly, jerking convulsively and panting like a runaway steam engine, Harold started to have a premature ejaculation.

Knowing that she'd never have a riper moment, Alison quickly shoved her hand under the mattress and brought out the hidden chair leg. She swung a terrific blow to the side of Harold's head. He rolled off her promptly with a sharp, strangled cry. Alison skipped nimbly out from under and hit him again on the back of the head as hard as she could. Harold lay still.

Simultaneously with Alison's efforts there came a tremendous growl and a baying roar from the tethered dog. He leapt at her with jaws wide open and all his hideous teeth in view. But the chain pulled him up short with an awful jerk and he rebounded, falling on his back. He was on his feet again, leaping and straining with demonic ferocity to get to her.

The chain held, but the roof timbers creaked alarmingly from the powerful exertions of the hound. Alison shrank away in terror. She knew instinctively that in order to be successful in her getaway bid she ought to beat the dog's brains out with her chair leg, but she was utterly incapable. Her capacity for violence was spent with the clobbering of the wretched Harold.

She threw the chair leg down, picked

up the hurricane lamp and ran out of her prison, shutting the door behind her to muffle the frenzied yelling of the dog. She found her way through two more store rooms in the loft, and then she came to the ladder which led down to the ground floor. The coach-house door was unlocked and there was nobody about as she found her way out into the cobbled courtyard of the old manor house. Faintly she could still hear Rufus going berserk back in the depths of the coach-house.

Still carrying the lantern to light her way, she started to run down the long, tree-lined drive. She'd worked it out that if she could once get to a road, even a 'B' road or a country lane, it wouldn't be long before she found a cottage or a passing motorist who could save her from those devils in the big house.

But the drive was nearly a mile long, and when she was only half way down it, to her horror she saw twin headlights suddenly swing into view and come racing towards her under the trees. It must be the criminals or their associates using the same van they'd used to transport her here. She certainly wasn't stopping to find out.

She climbed over the rusty iron fence into a field, extinguished the hurricane lamp, and started to run. She thought she heard a faint shout in the distance, so she increased her speed till she was sobbing for breath, her chest heaving painfully. She dare not go on a road now or they'd soon hunt her down with the vehicle. She was committed to running across country till she found help, or until the dog found her first.

She blundered through hedges, crashed through wet and dry ditches, snagged her clothes and lacerated her flesh on barbed wire in the darkness, but she hurtled on regardless. She was a good little sprinter in the school athletics team, and sheer terror increased her stamina.

The air was cold and damp with ghostly miasmas of mist rising from low-lying fields. There was no moon, and the countryside was pitch black, though Alison's eyes had become accustomed to the darkness and she could just see the outlines of trees and hedgerows. The eerie silence was broken occasionally by the sinister howl of some animal predator, or the wounded cry of a victim.

Alison ran lightly over the pasture land, and went round the edges of ploughed fields whose sticky furrows would have slowed her down.

'How much farther?' she thought despairingly. There wasn't a single light anywhere to offer her hope or succour in all this vast dark wilderness. She must have covered more than two miles across country when she saw a lighted window in the distance. But even as she gasped with relief she was promptly overwhelmed by terror and despair, for she heard on the night wind that source of all primeval fear to a fugitive, the distant baying of a savage dog. As she might have known, they'd sent that awful beast to hunt her down. The darkness was no shield against Rufus. She could hear his bawling venom as he hurried on her scent, and she'd never doubted he was a killer. She would be torn to pieces unless she reached that distant light before the dog overtook her. The criminals couldn't afford to let her live with what she knew.

In the middle distance on the top of a knoll she could now see the dark mass of a clump of trees, and she knew what she had to do. She could defeat the dog temporarily by climbing one of the trees, and trust to luck that somebody else would find her before the criminals did. It was her only hope.

The ferocious baying had grown twice as loud in a few minutes, which meant Rufus was overhauling her fast. She floundered in a watery ditch, clawed her way up a bank and rebounded painfully off a strand of rusty barbed wire. She crawled under it, regardless of lacerations, and stumbled against the smooth bark of a large beech tree. Feeling upwards for a handhold, she seized a branch and hauled herself off the ground. Dangling crazily for a moment in mid-air, she found a temporary foot-hold on a gnarled protu-berance and propelled herself upward.

Being city-bred, Alison had little experience of tree-climbing, and her blind panic made the operation even more hazardous. Upward she went in the pitch dark, regardless of her precarious hand-holds and her slipping feet, desperate to put as great a height as possible between herself and the killer hound.

Meanwhile the tenant farmer of these acres, John Jessop, who'd been anxiously patrolling his domain worrying about his sheep ever since he heard that blood-curdling yell of the killer dog in the distance, had come round the edge of the wood and entered the field which Alison had just crossed. He'd been having trouble of late from a sheep-worrying dog that roamed loose in the countryside at night. One or two of his sheep had been badly mauled by this unidentified beast. One ewe had broken her legs and had to be destroyed after being panicked into crashing through a hedge and down a steep embankment.

Farmer Jessop was hoping one night to catch that dog in *flagrante delicto* and dust his arse with buckshot to prevent any more losses in his flock.

He cocked his shotgun as he heard the savage, growling whine of the dog drawing near its kill, and suddenly Jessop was frightened by what was bearing down on him. He realised before he flashed his torch on it that this creature was something far more than a furtive sheep worrier. No man could control it or stand against it. Without his gun he would have been a dead man.

The great brute thrust his way hungrily through a thicket, his nose to the ground, following Alison's scent. Then Farmer Jessop shone his electric torch, revealing the great black body, the blunt head, tiny ears and appalling jaws of the Dobermann.

As Rufus became aware of his enemy standing before him, a hideous paean of triumphant rage bellowed from his throat. With salivating jaws wide open he leapt at his prey. Farmer Jessop had no time to deliberate. He dropped the torch, raised the gun to his shoulder and fired at the charging beast, feeling as hopelessly exposed as a big game hunter facing an attacking lion, who doesn't give you the chance for a second shot.

Fortunately for Jessop his hurried aim was good. The charge of buckshot smashed into the broad chest of the attacking dog barely five yards away, cutting him down in mid-flight, smashing flesh and bone and vital organs. As the dog collapsed with a pitiful whimper and thrashed about wildly in agony, Farmer Jessop fired his second barrel at the broad black head and finished Rufus off altogether.

Meanwhile Alison, clinging on precariously fifteen feet up in the beech tree across the field, heard the double boom of the shotgun and promptly concluded it was the criminals shooting at her. She started in terror, missed her footing and overbalanced, failing to find a handhold in the dark. She crashed down through the branches to the leaf-strewn earth beneath, with one leg twisted up under her, and struck her head on a gnarled old root pushing up through the soil. There was an awful stab of pain right through her body, a numbing shock and a blinding flash. She lost consciousness not knowing that help was so close at hand.

Farmer Jessop picked up his torch to have a closer look at the corpse of the huge dog which had come so close to killing him. Muttering indignantly about the maniacs who would give house room to such a dangerous beast, the farmer went striding off to report the incident to the police.

14

It was Davinia Brutnell, driving alone in the Dormobile van, whom Alison had encountered in the drive. Davinia had been on a shopping spree into Leatherhead, signing cheques that were sure to bounce in all the best shops

She was bored to distraction at being buried alive in the country, waiting for the Norman jackpot to materialise. Not that she really believed it would ever happen now. Ever since Godaseth had rung her from a call-box in Guildford, describing how the police had traced the Norman connection through his natural mother, and had grilled him ineffectually for forty-eight hours about the kidnapping, Davinia had been afraid.

She did not share Arthur's arrogant contempt for the police, or his easy optimism that the ransom could still be collected from Norman at a later date, since nobody was ever going to trace

Alison to her isolated prison. Davinia secretly believed that they should now cut their losses and abort the enterprise. They should release Alison unharmed in some lonely place and forget the whole scheme while there was still no hard evidence against them.

But she dare not voice her fears to Arthur, who was more frantically determined than ever to extract a fortune in negotiable currency from his victims, and kill Alison if he was thwarted.

If Davinia had ever convinced herself in the early days of their relationship that she was the dominant partner, she knew now bitterly that she was fooling herself. She had seen herself decline rapidly to the status of Godaseth's junior accomplice. She had watched him become more coldly ferocious, more madly egocentric and sadistic since that night when the crusade of violence first began in Dulwich. She couldn't control him now, and she was afraid. If she crossed him or stood in his way, her own life wouldn't be worth much.

When Davinia suddenly saw the little

wraith-like figure caught in the glare of her headlights like a moth far away down the long, ghostly drive, she was incredulous. It couldn't possibly be Alison, and yet how could it be anyone else in that place at that time? It was too early in the evening for Davinia to have been at the gin. She usually kept off the hard stuff when she was going to drive, for she knew how much depraved pleasure it would give the pigs to have her blow into their obscene little plastic bag and turn it green.

Davinia's doubts were roughly dispelled when the little figure in the distance suddenly vaulted over the low iron fence like an acrobat, and disappeared into the darkness. The hostage had escaped! What the hell had that fool Harold been doing to let her get out, and where was the dog?

She increased her speed and skidded to a violent halt in the manor courtyard. Then she heard the muffled baying of the dog from deep inside the coach-house, and she knew Alison must be a very cunning little bitch indeed.

Davinia grabbed her electric torch and hurried up to the loft. The dog quietened down a bit as she spoke to him, for she'd known Rufus as a puppy four years ago when he was being trained by Harold as a guard dog, and he still acknowledged Davinia as one of the good guys.

She stared with incredulous horror and fury at the macabre scene in Alison's former prison; at Harold lying uncon-scious on the old mattress, with his trousers round his knees, his cock exposed, and a rivulet of blood trickling down from his broken head. No sign of Alison.

'So that's what's been going on, you filthy little moron,' she raged, kicking the uncomprehending Harold in the ribs. 'Get up, you half-wit! Get up! Can't I trust you to do anything right?'

But Harold lay still, breathing stertor-ously through his open mouth, oblivious of the kicks and the voice of authority.

Davinia panicked at the thought of Alison getting clear away to tell somebody else of her kidnapping and imprisonment at the manor house. She had to be caught and silenced at once. There was only one infallible way to stop her and kill her with one move.

Davinia patted the eager, slobbering dog and released the choker chain from his throat.

'Go, Rufus!' she hissed. 'Seek and kill. Good boy. Kill!'

Rufus didn't need telling twice. With little yelps of savage excitement, his nose to the ground on Alison's scent, he was through the loft, down the steps and streaking away down the drive, leaping over the iron railings at a bound where Alison had taken to the fields. Davinia followed panting in his wake. She had to trail him somehow and be in at the kill, so that she could get Arthur here and somehow the corpse could be hidden before daylight. It would never do to have Alison found so close to the manor house with her throat torn out, for the police would soon be mounting a major search operation to find out who owned a dog capable of such ferocity.

Davinia soon found she wasn't really fit for this kind of cross-country endurance test. Too much booze, too many bedrooms, and too many cosseted years as a wealthy woman had made her soft and short of breath. But she was fortunate in that she'd been wearing her flat-heeled comfortable shoes for driving. She was goaded on by a terrible urgency to find and extinguish in Alison the testimony that could put Davinia in prison for a good many years.

She had her electric torch which was a great help in climbing over fences and finding gates or gaps in the hedge to go through. She followed the vengeful howling of the dog through the dark countryside until he was so far ahead that she could hardly hear him above the pounding of her own heart and the roaring of the blood in her ears.

She blundered on, as desperate as Alison had ever been, to meet that rendezvous with death. She heard a new crescendo of savage excitement from the dog, telling her that he'd found his prey. Then came that clear, startling double boom of the shotgun, and the dog's snarling roar ceased abruptly.

Davinia froze with horror, for she knew exactly what had happened. Some trigger-happy peasant had just shot Rufus. But she couldn't tell whether it was before or after he'd dealt with Alison.

Whatever had happened out there, Davinia saw no point in going on any further. Some outsider was already involved and it was therefore time for Davinia to bring up reinforcements. With deep gloom and foreboding she plodded back to the manor house, picked up the hall telephone and dialled Lisvane Theological College, asking the student operator on his night stint at the switchboard if she could speak to Mr. Godaseth.

'Who's that speaking, please?' said the virtuous young acolyte anxiously, for students were forbidden to take calls from women other than their close relatives.

'I'm his mother,' said Davinia arrogantly. 'It's rather important. Please hurry.'

So Godaseth, who'd just gone into the dining hall after Vespers, and was taking his frugal nightly sustenance of watery cocoa and a plain biscuit before retiring to his spartan cell, was summoned to the telephone. He took the call in the cubicle of the pay phone which adjoined the basement lavatories, and he wasn't very pleased with Davinia for he knew in his bones that a call at this hour could only mean bad news.

'Arthur,' she said curtly. 'Disaster. The worst. The package is away. That fool Harold. You must come at once.'

'Christ Almighty!' he blasphemed. 'What! How could it happen? What the hell were you doing, you bloody fool?'

'Get over here quickly. No time for post-mortems now. It could be too late already.'

She rang off, and Godaseth was raging and blaspheming like a docker as he deliberated what to do. He knew that detectives had been watching the college closely ever since his arrest and release, hopefully waiting for him to lead them to his hideaway. The cretins! You couldn't very well miss the pretentiously mediocre-looking car strategically sited in the road opposite the main gates to the college, so that its occupants could scan the faces of all students who left the college legitimately, and also have an oblique view of the west wing and Godaseth's cell window on the first floor. It was adequately bathed in the glow of the flanking sodium street lights a hundred yards away, so that anybody climbing out of a west wing window could be clearly seen by the watching detective.

But Godaseth had foresight and resource, and there was still another card up his sleeve. He'd pioneered an emergency escape route on the other side of the college, well clear of the policeman's field of vision. It was in the bath-house located in the east wing, in one of the shower cubicles. A small square window with an iron grille over it gave access to the shrubbery, and Godaseth had already eased and lubricated the screws holding in the bars, in readiness for such an emergency. Even when he'd removed the grille, it needed extreme agility and strength and a snake-like litheness to haul himself up and squeeze naked through the narrow aperture, having pushed out his clothes and shoes beforehand.

Godaseth negotiated it successfully, and ran quickly across the darkened lawns and tennis courts to the residential street which flanked the college grounds. In one of these staid Victorian villas there lived the widow of an old college servant, and Godaseth had hired the lock-up garage alongside the house. The woman was partly blind and totally deaf, and was glad enough of the pound a week which the nice young student gave her for the use of her otherwise useless garage.

Here Godaseth kept his motor cycle, a Honda Flat Four, 1000 c.c. machine which he'd stolen in Central London in preparation for the kidnapping campaign, so that no hired machine could ever be traced back to him. It worked out a good deal cheaper than hiring.

Within half an hour of receiving Davinia's phone call, he was at the manor house, angrily confronting her with her fatal incompetence.

'It wasn't my fault,' she countered with equal heat. 'I always looked on Harold as a retarded eunuch. How was I to know he'd nursed a secret obsession for nymphets all these years? The dirty little bitch cock-teased him, and then coshed him with a blunt instrument while he was trying to get it in. Absolutely typical of the cheap little scrubbers of today. No pride.'

'Never mind your bloody alibi,' he raged. 'We've got to find her before she gets near any police station, or she can get us put away for good. Can you find your way back along the route you were following when you heard the shots?'

'Yes, I'm sure I can. But isn't it too late for that? Shouldn't we get away from here at once, use the time to cover as much distance as possible?'

'Not till we've had a damned good try at finding the bitch. She may be lost in the dark, hiding there, afraid to move till daylight. With any luck she may even be hurt. If we scour the area thoroughly we could flush her out. Come on. We've got ten hours of darkness before anything can happen. Once she's dead and disposed of, there's no case against us. We can live to mount another snatch in a month or two.'

Armed with an electric torch apiece the gruesome pair hurried back over the fields in the wake of Alison and Rufus. Occasionally they were encouraged by the sight of a tuft of red wool on some barbed wire, where Alison had snagged her jersey in her desperate hurry to get through. Sometimes a frantically forced gap through a hedge with strands of wool on the thorns showed where she'd been.

At last they came to the very gap in the hedge where Rufus had burst through to attack Farmer Jessop. A few yards into the field their torches picked out the grim black bloodstained carcase of the shot Dobermann, lying where the farmer had left it. Contorted in death, Rufus looked almost supernaturally hideous.

Davinia shuddered, and murmured: 'Poor old Rufus. He didn't deserve that. He was only doing his job.'

Godaseth cursed violently.

'The swine's bound to report this to the police. Once they start asking questions round here, there's bound to be some big-mouthed yokel who'll tip them off that you had a Dobermann at the manor.'

'Will that matter? We'll be long gone from here by then,' said Davinia.

'You're a model of fortitude and endurance, aren't you?' sneered Godaseth. 'Well, I don't concede defeat till my nose gets rubbed in it. Come on, we'll hide the body so the dumb pigs won't believe there ever was a Dobermann, except in that yokel's drunken imagination. If there's no body, the fuzz will soon lose interest.'

He raised the big carcase by the forelegs and instructed Davinia to take the hind legs. Between them, with frequent pauses for rest, they carried Rufus's dead weight across two fields till they came to a deep ditch under a hedge. Here they tumbled him in and covered him over with sticks, stones and tussocks of grass till not even a whisker was visible. Only a concentrated body search of the area would ever bring him to light.

'Now to do the same for that little bitch,' said Godaseth with fiendish anticipation. 'I'm going to search that wood near where the dog was shot. It would be the logical place for her to make a dash for when he was getting close. You go and tackle them at that cottage,' he told Davinia, pointing to the solitary light across the fields that Alison had been making for when she first heard the dog in pursuit. 'It's possible she could have gone there for help. You can soon bounce them into handing her over, whatever yarn of hysterical paranoia she's spun them. Put on your Duchess Lady-of-the-Manor act. Say she's your mentally retarded niece who's seriously disturbed and enjoys inflicting mayhem on all her loved ones by running off across the fields at night with some crazy, mixed-up notion of persecution. They'll believe you when they know you come from the manor. It's a far more plausible tale than Alison's. Signal with the torch if she's there, three long flashes and three short. I'll do the same if I find her first.'

Increasingly disheartened by the turn events were taking, yet not daring to object or disobey him in his present murderous mood, Davinia plodded off across the fields towards the distant light, while Godaseth made for the wood where Alison had sought refuge.

* ★ * ★ * ★

Badly stunned and shocked by her fall, Alison slowly recovered consciousness and wondered where she was. Then it all came back to her with a tremendous wave of fear and despair. The darkness under the trees was so intense that she couldn't tell whether she was blind or not. She was chilled to the bone, and all her flesh was cold and clammy with the sweat of shock. There was a dreadful pain in her head, and she felt so ill that she was convinced she must be dying. She tried to sit up, and then such a ghastly spasm of pain shot through her left leg that she cried out involuntarily. She knew her left leg must be badly injured, probably broken, but she also knew that she couldn't stay where she was. She never doubted that the criminals would come looking for her and would kill her when they found her.

She couldn't really understand why the dog, whose horrific menace once loomed so large for her, had suddenly faded from her world without doing her any harm. But she was slowly working it out that the gunshots which had startled her into falling must have something to do with the sudden taming of Rufus.

By sheer will-power, enduring the agony like someone put to the torture, she edged her way deeper into the wood an inch at a time, resting to ease the unbearable pain in her leg, and then pushing on. She lost count of time and distance, until to her horror she thought she heard a faint human voice in the distance, somebody calling her name.

Almost paralysed with terror she knew beyond any doubt that it was *his* voice, the evil sound that would haunt her till she died.

'Alison, Alison, you can come out now. This is the police. We've caught those devils. Nobody's going to hurt you any more. It's all over. We've come to take you home and put you in a nice warm bed.'

Her panic was now so powerful that she hardly noticed the pain as she dragged herself onward at twice her former speed.

His voice was now quite loud, and she could hear him crashing through bushes and dead bracken in the wood. She was close to total despair, when she felt herself slip down a small grassy slope into a hollow, and needle-sharp thorns tore at her hands and face. She'd fallen into a disused and collapsed rabbit warren which led a good way underneath a huge bramble bush. She fought and wriggled frenziedly and wormed her way right under it, regardless of the malicious thorns tearing at her clothing and flesh from every side. Then she collapsed, quivering with pain and exhaustion, jamming her fist into her mouth to prevent herself from crying out with hysterical anguish and despair.

The rustling, impatient footsteps were now quite close. She could even see the eerie, reflected glow of his torch beam on the trees through her tangled roof of brambles. Godaseth was practically cooing to her now with concern and affection to come on out and be saved from all her miseries. She almost wished she could.

She heard him go past within ten yards of her blackberry bush, and could hardly believe he'd fail to see her red jersey under the brambles. He still seemed sure she was in hiding not far away.

'Police, Alison,' he called soothingly. 'It's all right now. Your friends are here. Your daddy's waiting in the pub at Cobham. Shout if you can hear me.'

Shortly afterwards the glow from his torch faded away and his crashing footsteps could no longer be heard. He'd gone away over the fields to look for her in other woods and copses.

Alison lay still, petrified with fear and immobilised by pain. Even if she could have dragged her injured leg any further, she knew she'd never have the courage to move from there while that revolting swine was anywhere about.

Then it started to rain, and within minutes she was soaked to the skin.

15

Next morning when Scamp arrived at Squad H.Q. in Bermondsey, Detective Inspector Earwacker was waiting for him with a glint of ill-suppressed excitement in his eye.

'I've just had a call from Detective Chief Inspector Gilbert in Leatherhead. He's co-ordinating that check-up on dog-owners and breeders in that part of Surrey where we think the Norman kidnappers may be holed up. He says the local constabulary at Cobham report an incident last night of a dog being shot in self-defence by a farmer.'

'What sort of dog?'

'He reckons it was a Dobermann and very fierce, a man-killer. A male dog, over a hundred pounds in weight.'

'He reckons?' said Scamp. 'Doesn't he know? Doesn't anybody down there recognise a Dobermann when he sees one?'

'Unfortunately,' said Earwacker, 'although the farmer claims to have shot him, there's no body to recognise.'

'What!'

'When this farmer went back with the village bobby, first thing this morning, to the field where he reckons he shot the Dobermann, the corpse had vanished into thin air. It had rained rather a lot in the night, so that any possible traces of blood on the grass had been washed away. There was nothing. The local policeman was very sceptical. He's not actually calling the farmer a liar, but he wonders if he was exaggerating a bit. Maybe it was an old dog fox or some stray mongrel that he saw in the field, and fired at him but didn't kill him. This farmer's known to be uptight about rogue dogs worrying his sheep.'

'But that's a bloody stupid view to take!' exclaimed Scamp incredulously.

'Is it? You should know by now how the police mind works, Scamp. No evidence means no further action. How many mares' nests would your professional life have been swallowed up in if you'd acted flat out without any corroborative evidence on every gobbledegook report from the well-meaning public?'

'But this is different altogether, guv,' protested Scamp. 'Cobham's right in the area we marked out as the operational zone for Alison Norman's kidnappers, and we know for sure the dog they're guarding her with is a Dobermann. If this farmer reckons he shot one right there in the target area, I for one am prepared to believe him. Why would he say Dobermann unless he knew it was one? Why not Alsatian or Saint Bernard or Irish Wolf Hound?'

'But why would the body disappear without trace during the night?' objected Earwacker sceptically.

'I don't know, guv. But there's something weird going on down there. You can bank on it. That Dobermann being loose in the countryside at all, tearing about after blood and attacking a farmer, could mean that things are starting to fall apart for the kidnappers. There should be a police dragnet put through the whole area as a matter of the utmost urgency. The

Regional Crime Squad down there should be knocking on doors at every farm and cottage, searching every empty or derelict building within a five-mile radius of where that dog was shot. Can't you ginger them up a bit, guv? That girl, if she's still alive, could be in danger, and this looks to me like a chance to find her. But it could be touch and go. There's not much time left.'

'You could be right,' conceded Earwacker, still sceptical. 'If you feel so strongly, why don't you go down there right away and tell Gilbert as tactfully as you know how that we consider this report of a shot Dobermann is a real crisis in the Alison Norman case, and justifies a major search of the whole district?'

'I wish I could, guv. But I'm in court at ten o'clock. Ivor Wilkes, the porn merchant. Crown Court.'

'All right then,' replied Earwacker resignedly. 'I'll go there myself and get things moving, just in case you are right about this kidnapping coming to a head.'

'You'll have to fight hard for it, guv, and get the Brass behind you. They're under-manned and over-pressured down there in the sticks, and I bet they don't take kindly to being told what to do by us.'

★　★　★

Alerted to the possibility of a big success by D. I. Earwacker, the Regional Crime Squad in Surrey burst into swift activity. Conducting a thorough routine search of buildings in the neighbourhood where Farmer Jessop had reported shooting a Dobermann, a carload of detectives drove up the long approach to the old manor house.

They found the aged and decrepit owner, Mr. Rupert Skeffington, sitting aimlessly among his souvenirs in a damp, dusty and cluttered room that belonged in the 1930's. The whole house was so neglected and decaying that mushrooms would soon be sprouting from the walls. The old man wanted to know if the war had broken out yet, and if that damned feller was still on the moon, but otherwise they could elicit no coherent response from him.

Hanging behind the door in the old-fashioned barn-like kitchen, they found Godaseth's Hell's Angel gear: black leather jacket, black crash helmet and black motor cyclist's boots. They also found his working cassock which was stained near the front opening with blood and semen. This boded ill for the girl victim, and spurred on the crime squad with even more desperate urgency to find her.

They started searching the outbuildings, and soon came to the suite of rooms above the coach house where Alison had been kept prisoner. Here they discovered a very old peasant woman called Ada Smith — a faithful retainer, as old as Skeffington himself, who'd lived and worked at the manor all her life — with thin white hair, a heavily wrinkled face like an old brown walnut, and small black eyes like rheumy, bloodshot blackberries. She was keening quietly to herself and dropping tears over her boy, a thin, small, middle-aged man with a face like a ferret's. He was flaked out on an old mattress with a fractured skull, and the old woman was trying to revive him by rocking him in her arms like a child.

The detectives questioned her sternly about Alison, and after much patient persuasion and hectoring they finally got her to admit that a young girl had indeed been living there in that loft for a week or two, but she didn't know who it was.

When had the girl gone?

She didn't know.

Who brought her there?

'It must be Miss Davinia,' said the old woman.

'Who is Miss Davinia?'

'She'll be coming back to live here, like it was in the old days. The master will be pleased.'

The detectives swiftly concluded that neither Ada Smith nor her employer was sufficiently *compos mentis* to have any idea of the kidnapping conspiracy that had been put into effect here over Alison Norman. The fact that Alison had now disappeared, together with the criminals who'd brought her here, suggested either that she'd escaped, or had been hurriedly moved to a new hiding place when danger of discovery threatened.

The fracas in which Harold Smith had had his head broken was something they couldn't quite explain, though there were all kinds of fanciful theories advanced.

The local police soon filled them in on the background of the owners of the manor house. Rupert Skeffington, octogenarian scion of an old county family, had inherited the place from his father, and lived there all his life, looked after by one old woman servant called Ada Smith, and her backward son Harold, who was good with animals. Skeffington used to breed dogs and horses, with Harold as his right-hand man. There had been three Skeffington children born and brought up at the manor: a son called Roger who was now farming in Rhodesia, and two daughters, Davinia Blanche and Susan Katherine, generally known as Kitty. Davinia had married a city merchant banker called Brutnell, and Kitty was some kind of a high-class drop-out.

A swift enquiry despatched to the Criminal Records Office at Scotland Yard brought the information that Davinia had form; convictions for drug offences, breaches of the currency regulations, and keeping a disorderly house.

Kitty had recently been in court for insulting behaviour and assaulting the police on the picket line at a North London factory which was in dispute with a trade union. It was fairly obvious that Kitty was just a simple-minded fuzz-hater, while it was Davinia who, according to Ada Smith, had lately returned to the manor after long years away, bringing with her a young girl who was to be accommodated in the loft.

Meanwhile, on the insistence of Detective Inspector Earwacker, who was making a big nuisance of himself at the Regional Crime Squad Headquarters in Leatherhead, dog-handlers and police reinforcements had been brought into the area to make a thorough ground search of that locality where Farmer Jessop still vehemently maintained that he'd shot the disappearing Dobermann.

At midday they started combing the wood where Alison had taken refuge. Thus it came about that Alison, soaked to the skin, numb with cold, unable to move her cramped limbs, half dead with shock, exposure and exhaustion, heard a rustling sound and opened her eyes to see the black and brown face of a police Alsatian staring curiously into her face.

Alison was convinced it was Rufus, come for her at last. Her demented screams brought the dog's handler and three other rubber-booted policemen running to the bramble bush.

16

Scamp left the Crown Court at three p.m. with the satisfaction of having seen the accused porn merchant found guilty and sentenced to two years.

When he arrived back at his office he found D. I. Earwacker, who'd just returned from his safari into Surrey, practically crowing like a rooster with jubilation.

'We found her,' he proclaimed triumphantly, 'not all that far away from where the farmer insists he shot a Dobermann. I had a gut feeling that dog was no fantasy. He was tracking somebody, so it had to be Alison.'

'How is she?' asked Scamp.

'Alive, just about. She fell out of a tree and broke her leg, a green-stick fracture. She's suffering from shock and exposure, as well as having been sexually assaulted by that Hell's Angel creep in his cassock.'

'Godaseth.'

That's still to be proved, so don't go

jumping the gun. The doctors say she's going to be all right — if any adolescent girl is ever all right after being well raped by a holy roller. She's in the General Hospital at Leatherhead. Her parents are with her, and they're over the moon. They're even prepared to forgive us for all our ham-fisted incompetence. They never thought they'd see her again, never mind get her back alive. So we really do have some satisfied customers for a change. It was a pretty close-run thing though. If I hadn't raised hell till they brought in some dog-handlers to comb that particular area, it would have been too late. She was too far gone to move with her broken leg. Another hour or two where she was, soaked to the skin under a bramble bush, and she'd have been dead from exposure.'

'Well, a bit of success now and again never did anybody any harm,' observed Scamp. 'All we've got to do now to tidy everything up and close the case is bring in the villains who planned this snatch.'

'Well, I've every confidence in your

251

ability to bring that off,' replied Earwacker, as if the case no longer concerned him.

★ ★ ★

When Alison was sufficiently recovered and able to receive visitors, Scamp went to see her in the hospital at Leatherhead. He was impelled not so much by curiosity to see the girl victim who'd beaten all the odds by escaping from ruthless captors and surviving to turn the tables on them, as to assess her potency as a witness. He was afraid that a highly competent defence counsel was going to make a big issue of the identification of Godaseth. Scamp wondered how effective Alison was going to be when she was being hectored and brow-beaten in the witness box at the Old Bailey by an exhibitionist Q.C., determined to make his name by securing an acquittal in a highly publicised and controversial case.

Alison was in a clean, bright, flower-bedecked private room equipped with telephone, television and every other material comfort, for Donald Norman had spared no expense on the daughter returned from the dead.

There was a uniformed police constable on duty outside the door to repel the eager reporters from the national newspapers, who couldn't wait to get Alison's exclusive story. 'How I was raped by the man in black' was a main headline already blocked out by one popular tabloid.

The presence of the policeman was also a solemn reminder that Alison's kidnappers were still at large.

Alison was sitting up in bed reading. Characteristically she was reading *Pride and Prejudice*, one of the set books for her 'A' Level English course. She looked very young, innocent and immature. Her face was small and plain and unmarked by the savagery of her experiences, though there was a certain wariness and cynicism in her eyes far in advance of her age. The plaster cast on her leg was the only physical evidence of her ordeal.

Scamp found himself marvelling, not for the first time, at the extraordinary survival powers of seemingly frail women.

'Who are you?' said Alison bluntly.

Scamp introduced himself and explained that he'd been working on her case in London.

'Well, thank you for trying to find me,' she said tartly, 'but you weren't very good at it, were you? If I hadn't got away on my own, I'd still be there, waiting till they decided to kill me.'

Scamp had to admit that she was probably right. He detected that she was bubbling over with pride and self-congratulation in her achievement at escaping from the criminals, killer dog and all. If she'd ever lacked confidence in her life before, she had plenty of it now. It gave her a self-perpetuating euphoria that went far towards cancelling out the hideous trauma of the imprisonment, the terror and the rape.

'Have you caught them yet?' she said.

'No, they're on the run, but every policeman in the country is looking for them. They won't get far.'

'That swine who raped me, all got up in a black hood and cassock to frighten me. The other detective told me he was poor Helen's illegitimate son. No wonder she killed herself, knowing she'd given birth to a creature like that. But why didn't she tell somebody she knew it was him, if she was going to kill herself anyway? Why was she prepared to let me go on suffering?'

'A woman's loyalty to her only son,' said Scamp. 'Don't knock it too much. We soon got on to him by other enquiries and brought him in for questioning. But we hadn't got a scrap of evidence to charge him with, and he lied in his teeth with a good lawyer at his elbow. So we had to let him go.'

'How stupid!' said Alison contemptuously. 'Why didn't you beat the truth out of him, as they'd have done in a civilised country like France or America?'

'A good question,' said Scamp drily. 'I don't have the answers. You'd better talk to the psychologists and sociologists.'

'I'll tell you this much,' she exclaimed fiercely. 'No man's ever going to get me like that again. As soon as my leg's mended I shall go to karate and judo classes, and get a black belt. I'll carry a stiletto concealed in my bra and castrate any other swine who tries it on.'

'That's good thinking,' Scamp applauded. 'I'm sure you will, if the job you did on poor old Harold Smith's skull is anything to go by.'

'What will they do to that woman, the bitch who owned the manor house?'

'She'll get a cell like a battery hen's in Holloway Gaol for a few years,' said Scamp. 'She'll have a rough time there too with her top-drawer accent and snooty manners. The prison officers will really love her. So will the other cons.'

'Serve her right. I hope they brand her with a hot iron.'

'When the trial comes up,' said Scamp, 'if this man goes on steadfastly denying it was him, and you can't pick him out because you never saw his face, the defence will make a big play on the question of identity. If there should be reasonable doubt about nailing him down to the crime, he could be acquitted.'

'Don't worry about that,' said Alison confidently. 'I'll identify him for you. If there were a dozen men lined up, all the same size, dressed in hoods and cassocks, I could pick out the swine who raped me.'

'How?'

'By his eyes,' said Alison. 'I always looked at his eyes. They were very dark and crazy, and they sort of glowed with his madness. I've never seen a man with eyes like that before, so it's no good him trying to hide from me behind his black hood.'

'Well, that's a relief anyway.'

'I can pick him out by his voice as well,' said Alison. 'You get twelve men with him among them, put them in the next room where I can hear but can't see them, and get them to read out a short sentence, one at a time. I'll know his voice as soon as I hear it.'

'Any particular sentence?' said Scamp.

'Yes, this one: 'You can bleed, you little bitch, for all anybody cares.' Make them all say that, because his voice gets a certain vibration that nobody else's has, especially on the word 'bleed'.'

'That's very good,' said Scamp. 'I'm sure it'll be enough, with all the other evidence, to stitch him up if they try to wriggle out of it on grounds of mistaken identity.'

'Well, somebody has to be observant to catch these criminals,' said Alison patronisingly. 'You policemen obviously aren't very good at it.'

17

Godaseth and Davinia Brutnell were on the run, and the hunt was up. Their only hope of freedom was to leave the country, and in the long term their situation was hopeless. They'd need bent passports to get anywhere and avoid extradition later. Godaseth had no money, and Davinia's husband had died a bankrupt, so they must be penniless flotsam. They were hiding out somewhere, probably together, and the most strenuous police activity had so far failed to flush them. The usual snouts and underworld grape-vine were useless with these two, for they were right outside the normal criminal community and could probably look for help among the irreproachable.

Scamp wasn't disposed to wait about for months while the fugitives raised money from Davinia's wealthy friends and arranged an illicit departure on a small boat from one of the countless harbours and genteel yachting venues round the coast.

So he went after Davinia's sister Kitty, whose address was well known to the police after her squalid little affray on the North London picket lines. Scamp had a shrewd idea that Kitty, the trendy, progressive radical, Left Wing Women's Lib drop-out, would take a critical and contemptuous view of Davinia, the affluent hedonist who married merchant bankers and spared no thought for her poor, underprivileged brothers.

Kitty Skeffington was a tall, angular blonde in her late twenties, who worked voluntarily for a trendy charity in the East End on behalf of London's rootless and homeless flotsam. She smoked incessantly, swore like a navvy, and gave non-stop orders in her high falsetto deb's voice to all her bustling helpers.

'I don't normally talk to pigs,' she trilled in her fluty voice when Scamp introduced himself.

But on the subject of her elder sister Davinia, whom she'd always self-righteously despised, she was prepared to stretch a point some considerable way.

She ran scathingly through all Davinia's shortcomings, from the shameless seduction of the gardener's boy when she was fifteen, to her various marriages and divorces and profligate affairs with unsavoury men who were all rich, flashy, and irretrievably bent.

To Scamp's persistently recurring question as to whom Davinia was likely to approach for help when she was in trouble with the law, Kitty nominated decisively a South African financier in London called Piet Johannis Hoofhanger. Davinia had had a long drawn-out and sultry affair with him, and afterwards had always maintained a close connection, probably on a business-with-pleasure basis. If she needed help against the law, she wouldn't go to anyone else, asserted Kitty decisively.

With this information it was a fairly routine matter for Scamp and Earwacker to pay a visit to the financier at his Kensington home, and politely put it to him that he had too much to lose in risking a charge of obstructing the police and harbouring a suspect as hot as Davinia Brutnell now was.

At first the tough South African tried to bluster with the pretence that he didn't even know Davinia Brutnell. But when Scamp suggested that it might be necessary to put him on the Target Criminal File and have all his activities thoroughly investigated, Hoofhanger quickly capitulated.

A few days ago, he said, Davinia had come to him saying she needed somewhere quiet to stay with her friend, until a scandal in which she was involved had blown over. So he'd given her the key to his summer cottage in Sussex, and extended an invitation to stay there as long as she needed its privacy.

He wrote down the address of the cottage with a gold ball-point, and handed it over to Earwacker, after which he ushered them through his front door as solicitously as if they'd been Arab oil billionaires.

The two detectives went back to H.Q., where Earwacker drew a pistol from the armoury and rang up the County Police in Chichester, informing them as a matter of courtesy that he was coming down to interview a couple of suspects, believed to be living on their patch. He did not need any back-up reinforcement from the local police.

18

The two detectives drove as quickly as possible through the rush-hour traffic, southward out of London. It was getting dark and starting to rain as they passed through Kingston-on-Thames, but once past Guildford the traffic thinned out and moved faster along the A3. They were nearing Petersfield in little over an hour.

Hoofhanger's summer cottage was situated in the old village of Bosham, nestling on a quiet inlet of Chichester Harbour, where a deep channel gave access to the residents' yachts and motor cruisers to reach the open sea five miles away.

The road which ran along the shore in front of the houses was always under water at high tide, so the detectives had to drive a couple of miles round on country lanes to reach The Old Rectory, the large, rambling thatched house in its two-acre garden that Hoofhanger called his cottage. It stood on a knoll barely thirty yards from the water's edge, and at high tide you could hear the lapping of the wavelets on the muddy shore, while the yachts and dinghies rode so close at their moorings that you almost got the impression you were in among them.

There was a car, a fairly new Cortina, standing in the drive under the fir trees, and lights on in the downstairs rooms of the half-timbered house. Scamp lifted the bonnet and removed the rotor arm from the car's distributor, just in case of an attempted breakout, and then made his way round to the back to cover the rear exit.

Earwacker gave him time to get in position, and then pulled hard on the antique bell-handle.

The woman who came to the door was a sultry blonde, heavily made up, dressed in dark green slacks and sweater, with a cashmere shawl round her shoulders, and the whiff of expensive perfume mingling with the aroma of her French cigarette. She looked altogether too exotic to be in her natural surroundings in a holiday seaside house.

'Police,' said Earwacker curtly. 'Are you Davinia Brutnell?'

The woman stiffened as if deep-frozen. Being on the run had been disastrous for her nerves. The burden of isolation in this desolate hole had been crushing the life out of her, and she'd been living for days in dread of this moment.

'Oh my God!' she shrieked. 'It's the f - ing pigs! Arthur, run! Get going!'

There was a sound of violent movement in the interior, and all the lights went out as somebody threw the master switch. Earwacker, plunged in darkness on the doorstep, was aware of hurrying footsteps down the passage, and realised the woman had gone. He stepped inside the house and slammed the front door. There was a sudden eerie silence throughout the house as he waited, tense and nervous, for something to happen, knowing that there was a psychopath in the house who had nothing to lose by taking a life. It was one of those well-known occasions when Earwacker wished he was a long way off. He drew the short-barrelled Smith and Wesson from his shoulder holster, realising the position really was desperate when you had to come down to this.

Suddenly the light of an electric torch blazed out at him from the end of the passage, and instinctively he flung himself flat on the carpeted floor. A split second later there came the boom of one of Hoofhanger's sporting guns with which he shot mallard in the nearby creeks. A charge of game shot blasted down the passage to tear a jagged hole in the front door.

'Godaseth, you crazy bastard!' yelled the enraged Earwacker. 'That's worth another three years on top of your other sentence. Throw you gun down or I'll shoot. You haven't got a chance.'

He heard a door close hastily as the fugitive retreated before the threat of retaliatory fire.

Meanwhile round the back of the house, finding the kitchen door locked, Scamp had forced the sash on one of the old-fashioned leaded windows and climbed into a small sitting-room. He carried the electric torch while Earwacker carried the gun. Scamp never used a gun if he could avoid it, for he'd been shot once himself, and firearms gave him the horrors.

As he threaded his way between the articles of choice period furniture of the cluttered room, Scamp heard the shotgun go off on the other side of the door, followed by Earwacker's shout. It startled him out of his skin.

Scamp switched his torch out in case it attracted gunfire, and a second later he heard the door open urgently in the room where he was standing. He couldn't see a thing in the pitch black as a man stepped into the room and the door clicked shut. In the intense silence he could hear the distant whirring of a starter motor as Davinia Brutnell sought desperately to take off, not realising that Scamp had her rotor arm in his pocket.

With the intruder still unaware of his presence a few feet away from him, Scamp, who had a natural feeling for locations in the dark, suddenly hurled himself at the man by the door.

There was a startled yell as he collided

with a hard, muscular body, and the cold steel barrel of the shotgun caught him a numbing blow on the side of the face. Scamp grabbed at the weapon with one hand, and simultaneously drove his right hand, still holding the electric torch, at the centre of the man's body.

The other barrel of the gun went off, and Scamp was showered with plaster as it blew a hole in the ceiling. As his adversary keeled over from the body blow, Scamp delivered a downward thrust to the back of the neck, still using the torch as a club.

'That's worth a few Hail Mary's, you bastard,' said Scamp, taking out his handcuffs and switching on the torch to identify the dark hair and clean-cut, good-looking face of Arthur Godaseth, now breathing heavily in repose.

'Well, I'll be damned!' exclaimed Scamp. 'The bugger's still wearing his cassock, the new one.'

'Are you all right, Scamp?' said Earwacker, panting up to the scene. 'When I heard the other barrel go off, I thought you'd bought it. The bastard very nearly blew me away. If anybody ever needed topping it's him. He'll still be young enough to raise hell after he's served his time for this, and it's a racing certainty he's going to kill people.'

'Rehabilitation is the aim, guv,' said Scamp ironically. 'He'll be able to pray a good many years in his cell, and that can't be bad. What with all the shrinks who'll go to work on him, and the Open University at his finger-tips, he'll probably get paroled as a Doctor of Divinity.'

About the Author

P.A. Foxall is one of the most promising authors of crime and detective fiction to have appeared on the scene in many years. Combining a unique gift for dialogue with a devilish skill at devising intricate and suspenseful plots, Mr Foxall will undoubtedly be ranked with the most distinguished authors of suspense books. He has travelled throughout the world and spends his free time exploring new places, always searching for ideas for new novels.

THE SISKIYOU TWO-STEP

Richard Hoyt

John Denson, a private investigator, goes to Oregon's North Umpqua River to fish trout but, instead, he finds himself caught up in a net of international intelligence agents and academics. It all starts when the naked body of a girl with a bullet hole between her eyes goes rushing past Denson in the rapids. He embarks on a bizarre search to find the girl's identity and to bring her killer to justice. Strange clues lead to three more corpses, and only the Siskiyou Two-Step saves Denson from being the fourth . . .

THREE MAY KEEP A SECRET

Stella Phillips

The proudest citizens of Dolph Hill would not deny that it was a backwater where nothing ever happened — until, that is, the arrival of handsome, secretive Peter Markland disturbs the surface. After his shocking and violent death, old secrets begin to emerge. Detectives Matthew Furnival and Reg King are put on the case. As they delve through the conflicting mysteries, how will they arrive at the one relevant truth?